THE BEST OF

A. S. WEST

Three of West's

Most Popular

Short Stories

PLUS

Tales From The

Cryptid Library

THE BEST OF A. S. WEST

PUBLISHED BY
PSi Publishing

DEDICATED TO
My family:
Gree, Amidie, Alan, Ryan & Sally
and
Walt Lancaster, John Shaw
and
Martha & CeCi

TREE LOVERS

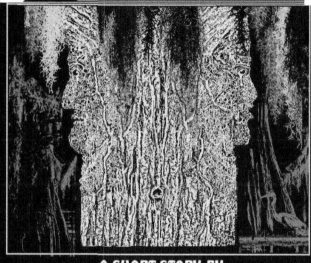

A SHORT STORY BY

A. S. West

INTRODUCTION

The swamps and marshes of Louisiana are beautiful sights to behold, but as sunlight fades and shadows grow long they become an eerie landscape filled with strange and unfamiliar sounds, a place where malevolent creatures roam and only the strong of heart prevail.

THE BEGINNING

The population of New Orleans doubled in the 1830's and by 1840, New Orleans had become the wealthiest city and third-most populous city in the nation behind New York and Baltimore, whose population exceeded New Orleans by only 100 people. Yet despite its wealth, its architecture, and its culture, its topography and its environment were inhospitable and uninhabitable, and thus undesirable for people to congregate, much less reside and populate...in large numbers.

Nonetheless, by 1840, New Orleans was 120-years old and had already established a vaunted history. Founded and ruled by the French, then the Spanish, and then reverting to the French again before being sold by Napoleon Bonaparte to the United States in 1803. A bright future lay ahead for the city. However, outside of the city was another thing. Outside of the city lay a brutal landscape. To be sure there were many plantations that lined the banks of the Mississippi, but most were up river from New Orleans. The farther inland one traveled the more undesirable the terrain.

Vast expanses of swamps, marshes and festering backwaters made New Orleans an island unto itself. And, since the dynamics of water is always to seek its own level, and as the city is at sea-level or below, water has been the nemesis that has plagued it since its founding. The endless wetlands around the city were inhabited by rogues and pirates, such as Jean LaFitte and his brother Pierre, and the occasional runaway slave or outlaw. Most inhabitants were rugged souls that eschewed the confines of city life preferring instead the open life the wetlands afforded them. Also living in these uncharted wetlands was a plethora of fauna and flora, and many exquisite and unique sites. There are also dangers one would face that city-dwellers couldn't imagine, dangers such as alligators, poisonous snakes, and spiders, black bear, panthers and wolves. And, according to legend, another creature more terrible than all the rest living there was the cruel "Loup-garou" or "Rougarou", a creature with the body of a human and the head of dog or wolf that feasts on the blood of humans.

The primary distinction between the Rougarou, known in other parts as "Dogman", and the European "Werewolf" is that Werewolves are like skin-walkers changing or morphing from human to wolf and back again. The Rougarou are creatures created as such and therefore, do not morph. Only the bravest and most experienced Trapper would have dared enter these swamps as they were known to swallow people up; people entered the swamps, never to be seen or heard from again. It was in this harsh environment lived an old Wizard aka, "Bokor" a Haitian term for a Vodou (Voodoo) priest or other practitioner who works with both the light and dark arts of magic it is believed that there are malevolent spirits contained in the form of various animals.

The old Wizard was widely known throughout the area, much like the eminent and influential Marie Laveau, the "Voodoo Queen" of New Orleans, who resided in the city. The Wizard, born Jean Auguste Tremain, was never referred to by his name, he was just the "Wizard". But, he was the most feared Wizard of all. It was reported that he could cast spells and even change people into animals or amphibians. It was also rumored that even the ferocious Loup-garou feared the old Wizard, giving him wide berth whenever venturing into his area of the great swamp.

The old Wizard only visited the city a few times a year to purchase supplies and other necessities such as salt, sugar, filé and other herbs, or seasonings he couldn't otherwise grow. He also sold to other practitioners of the arts- bats, newt's, parts of chickens he raised, snakes, salamanders, frogs and an assortment of eyes, tongues, feet and so forth that are used in preparing mojos, gris-gris, or magic charms to curse, bless, and/or to protect people. He always had a bagful of these tokens that he'd sell at a hefty price to the general populace, but to the substantial classes of mixed race, free people who were his primary customers, he bartered and traded only. They would seek him out luring him with smoked meats, vegetables, arts and crafts, pottery, and even clothing, in trade for his potent charms.

When he made these forays into the city he would often times be found in Congo Square, a place reserved for African traditions and expressions of culture and religion, including Voodoo. Congo Square was located on North Rampart Street between St. Anne and St Peter Streets, in the Tremé neighborhood. It was the only place where slaves were allowed to congregate every Sunday, to trade, sing, dance, and play music. The Wizard could also be found around Jackson Square as he liked to visit with vendors and, being Catholic, he also attended a mass or two at St. Louis Cathedral.

On one of these visits he was approached by a rich Creole man who was willing to pay a huge price for the purchase of a hex. Something that would curse a competitor, a free man of color, who was seeking to find favor with the royal Creoles who controlled much of the city, including some of the various exchanges in New Orleans which included the Louisiana Sugar and Rice Exchange as well as the Cotton Exchange and the Fruit & Vegetables Exchange. Much as exists today, fortunes could be made and lost depending upon one's position and timing in these exchanges.

When the Creole met the old Wizard he was accompanied by his daughter, a beautiful, young Creole girl whose almond colored skin, waxen black hair, and bright green eyes attracted anyone who happened to gaze upon her lovely visage. The Wizard was very much enamored by her. It could even be said, he was flirtatious in her presence. At the conclusion of their meeting, the Creole asked the Wizard what he owed him. The Wizard replied that when the hex had accomplished the Creole's intent, then and only then would he make known the payment requirement.

In a month's time, the competitor had been struck by a perplexingly odd fever and within the span of a week, was found dead. The Creole had some misgivings about his competitor's death, as he left a young widow and two small children, but he vowed that he should make it a point to make some provision for the young widow after he successfully completed his transactions.

As for now, however, he was over-come with joy. He also realized it was a bonus that his competitor had ceased being a competitor in every respect. The rich Creole contracted a Trapper friend whom he had known for many years and trusted implicitly. The Trapper was also very familiar with the wily old Wizard. The Creole commissioned the Trapper to summon the Wizard as he was ready to make payment to him. A week later, the Trapper informed the Creole that the Wizard would arrive in town on the next full moon.

On that night he was to come to Congo Square to meet him. And, as an added request, he was to bring his lovely daughter with him. As the full moon rose over Congo Square, the Creole found the old Wizard seated under a large live oak tree stirring the embers of a dying fire with a withered cypress stick. Seeing his approach, the Wizard rose and greeted the Creole and his daughter with a solemn bow of reverence. However, he did not extend his hand when the Creole offered his. The Creole took no offense, as he reasoned, that lord only knew what was on the Wizard's hands. Instead, he cordially greeted the Wizard, patting him on his shoulder, beaming over the events of his sudden good fortune.

"What do I owe you for your services, old man", the Creole intoned. "Name your price. No request will be denied." The old Wizard had settled himself back on his seat, poking the embers once again with his stick. The Creole again asked him for his price, a tone of annoyance in his voice. "Make known your price, old man. The moon has risen and people are beginning to gather. My daughter does not need to be exposed any longer to the night air. State your price that I may pay you and take our leave of this place." Without looking up the old Wizard said, "Your daughter. That is my fee. What?" The Creole exclaimed. Again the

Wizard replied, "Your daughter. Your daughter is my fee."

Thinking it a joke, the Creole let out a raucous bellow of laughter, but noticing how the Wizard was not laughing, his amusement quickly turned solemn as he paused to consider the old man's request. And, as the weight of the Wizard's words sank in, he bristled in anger. "Old man, you surely must be joking. You had best be joking, for there is nothing more precious to me than my daughter." Without looking up, the Wizard repeated, "Your daughter...that is my fee." Now enraged, the Creole shouted back, "I knew you were eccentric, you old fool, but you are out of your mind too, if you think for a minute I would give you my daughter; you are indeed crazy! Do you hear me old man?" The Wizard was unfazed and continued to poke at the fire.

The Creole bent over to glare into the Wizard's eyes, to drive home his point.

But the Wizard just stared into the flame, never shifting his gaze, as he continued to stoke the fire. The Creole was beside himself with fury. He wanted to tear the Wizard apart, limb from limb. In his rage he laid hold of the Wizard grabbing him by the lapels of his worn leather coat, and lifting him off the ground. He stared fiercely into the Wizard's eyes. Yet, before he could utter another word, his attention shifted as he became aware that the clamor of laughter, music, and conversation, had died suddenly. "Father!" urged the daughter. "We must go...now! We must leave this place." It was only then that the Creole took notice of the gathering of men and women encircling the big oak and the three people near the fire. Many in the crowd were armed with machetes or other edged weapons. No one uttered a word. They only stared fiercely at the Creole. Realizing that discretion was the better part of valor, and better to live and fight another day at his place of choosing. He released the Wizard, and slowly began backing away. Taking his daughter in hand while pointing with the other, he issued a stern warning, "You come near my daughter and I'll kill you old man. The crowd surged momentarily as if eager to attack the Creole, hacking him to death on the spot. The old Wizard simply shook out his coat...brushing his sleeves in a gesture of contempt and settled back down on his seat as if nothing had happened.

The rich Creole quickly departed from the area and the crowd dispersed. Soon the square was alive again with music and laughter.

Two nights later the daughter came down with a terrible fever. Cold compresses, cold baths, warm herbal teas; nothing would release her from the grips of the fever. Alarmed that his daughter was under a hex of some sort by the Wizard, the Creole sent the Trapper with word that if he released his daughter from the grip of fever he would consent to have her brought to him. The Trapper returned with the Wizard's response which was, the daughter would be free of the fever in two days' time. He would then expect the daughter's arrival in 10 days after healing. As the Wizard had prophesied, the fever was gone by the second day and she was up and drinking light tea with a biscuit.

The Creole explained to her what must happen, that for a brief moment she would have to be under the Wizards care, and living in his dwelling with him until he could devise a plan to dispose of the Wizard. As long as the Wizard remained alive, none of them were safe.   In the meanwhile, the father was making ready to deliver her to the Wizard with the proviso that he agreed to have the Creole's house boy on-site to insure that his daughter wasn't mistreated or abused in any way. The house boy had grown up with the daughter in the Creole's house. His mother had been the family cook for 30-years before succumbing to yellow in the last epidemic. His name was Tuloquit, pronounced, tah- Lou'-qee, an Indian name given to him by his grandmother, a free person of color who had married an Indian man whose family lived near the town of Toluquilla, Mexico, in the region near Guadalajara. The grandmother and the Indian were married aboard a slave ship bound for Haiti where Toluquit was born.

His family later escaped from the horrors of the Haitian Revolution in the diaspora, and arrived in New Orleans where he and his mother were taken in by the rich Creole man. Though the family was considered free people of color they lived a life as indentured servants to the Creole and his family. In return, they were provided a safe haven within the Creole's house located in the Marigny section of New Orleans, just down river from the French Quarter and near to the French Market, where they shopped daily for fruits and vegetables and all manner of food items for the Creole man's household. Over time Tuloquit and his mother became like family to the Creole and were devoted to the Creole and his daughter and well. The two children had been in one another's company since early childhood and had enjoyed a life of means growing up, attending school, playing every day, and running errands for the Creole's household.

The day they left New Orleans was a terribly sad day. Everyone in the house wept uncontrollably, especially the Creole. His daughter tried to comfort him, but he was inconsolable. He promised that he would do all in his power to have his daughter restored to the family as quickly as possible. And then among affectionate hugs and kisses they bid each other farewell. The old Trapper who had acted as emissary between the Creole and the Wizard was delivering them into the Wizard's care.

The Trapper stayed two days at the Wizard's meager home assuring him that all were well and safe, as safe as could be expected under the circumstances. Before the Trapper left he reminded the daughter that he would return every six weeks to check on her and to deliver fresh provisions. While there he would also be assured of her well-being. The first week or two were strange.

The Wizard lived in an old cabin that was in desperate need of repairs. The roof leaked and the clapboard siding had gaping holes large enough for any and all manner of insects to enter the dwelling. Toluquit busied himself with patching the cabin as best he could with the materials he had on hand. Meanwhile, the daughter worked inside to make the cabin more livable and comfortable. She and Toluquit put in a garden where she hoped to grow beans, peas, and legumes. In the afternoons she prepared the evening meal, which usually consisted of fried cornbread and whatever meat or vegetables were available. For desert she served wild berries or excellent fruit compost that she had learned at Toluquit's mother's knee. She also mashed berries finely into a smooth paste that could be spread on the cornbread. In addition, she had brought along a croc of thick, dark honey she had purchased recently at the French Market, which she would pour over warm, freshly baked cornbread.

It was a meager existence, but she was willing to do all she could to make it bearable until her father rescued her from this horrid place. The young couple even considered running away, but those thoughts were quickly dashed by the fact that they did not have any idea where they were. How could they possibly know which way to run? The vast, inhospitable swamp stretched for miles and miles in every direction. No, they decided, the best thing to do was to stay busy and help each day pass by as quickly and pleasantly as possible. At least they had each other to lean on. And the Trapper would be arriving with more provisions and news from home on his regular visitations.

The old Wizard never revealed to anyone the rationale behind requiring the daughter as payment from the Creole; however, it was simply a matter of love at first site. Though he never exhibited any emotions concerning the daughter, he was in a spell, not one cast by a purveyor of witchcraft or voodoo, but one cast by fate, with strong ties to the heart. He was at once in love with her upon first laying his eyes on her. The Wizard had never had a female companion, as he reasoned it would be a detriment to his craft to have a wife. However, now in his elder years he recognized a need for companionship and affection. Yet as someone new to the feelings that now controlled so much of his thoughts, he was susceptible to the ruination that envy and jealousy could wreak on a neophyte, such as himself. In the game of love, he had neither an idea of the rules, nor how to play.

However, as a result of his tender emotions towards his guest he had grown short-tempered, and was beginning to view Toluquit as a rival and not as a companion. He was accustomed to a life of solitude. He rarely had guests and he rarely traveled. He certainly wasn't used to having people, much less young people under foot all day. And, the constant chatter...only reinforced his view of life. No one should have that much to say in a day much less in an hour. To say that it was an adjustment for everyone was an understatement. Furthermore, he was jealous of Toluquit's relationship with the daughter. It wasn't so much that he wanted to engage in conversation with her, he just wanted her around, to be in his presence, but only when it was convenient. The old Wizard wasn't capable of a normal relationship. He has spent too many years in isolation. What he wanted and didn't know or couldn't articulate, was an object. Something beautiful, that belonged to only him, something he didn't have to share, something he could take down off the shelf and hold and admire, and then place back on the shelf to gaze lovingly at, whenever he chose.

He had begun questioning Toluquit's loyalty. He suspected that Toluquit was only there waiting for an opportunity in which he might attack and kill him. After all, the Creole had wanted to eliminate his competitor...was this really that different, especially in light of the heavy payment that he had paid? His mind ran away with his thoughts. He could no longer be in control of his emotions. He was beginning to think he had made a mistake bringing the girl here to live. But now that she was here he couldn't bear the thought of living without her. He had become a living, breathing paradox. It was only the beginning of the end.

The old Wizard's moods swings were becoming more volatile and animated. His animosity grew in leaps and bounds concerning Toluquit. It was so bad that he had barred Toluquit from the house, forcing him to take his evening meal outdoors on the porch, and forcing him to sleep in an old corn crib that was home to giant beetles and all manner of insects. Toluquit was soon covered with bites and stings. The Wizard would not permit the couple to be alone together. And, if they had to be together he had to be present. He wanted to be able to listen in on any conversation they had, but he had even placed restrictions on their conversations as well. Their incessant chatter was something the Wizard intended to harness. People weren't supposed to ramble idly all day. Speak when you need to say something, not when you want to say something, is what he said as a reminder

The young couple were stymied, they could not reason why the old Wizard was acting the way he was? These new demands required that Toluquit keep his guard up and be on the defensive whenever around the old man. Toluquit was there only to protect the Creole's daughter, but the old Wizard was now certain that the sole reason for Toluquit's presence was for the purpose of murdering him. One day his paranoia got the better of him and he attacked Toluquit with an iron rake, chasing him into the swamp a considerable distance before exhaustion overtook him. From this point on

Toluquit and the Wizard were on a crash course, a course that would only end badly for one or both of them.

Then, one fall morning the Wizard left early, saying only that he had some business to take care of and that he'd be home in time for the evening meal. The daughter and Toluquit were leery of the old man's intents, but decided to pursue their daily chores, nonetheless. Early in the afternoon, when they were finished with their chores Toluquit observed that the daughter was unusually sad. He knew she missed her father terribly, and, her home, which she had never been away from for more than a few days. Finally, she missed her life in New Orleans, the French Market, shopping at all the stalls and enjoying the hustle and bustle of city life. She wanted this nightmarish existence to end.

Noting her gloomy countenance, Toluquit went to comfort her. He held her in his arms and told her that everything would be alright. He said the Trapper was due any day and that he would be bringing news from home, along with a fresh supply of provisions. He knew that she was always happier after the Trapper had arrived. As youth are sometimes wont to do, they don't always think things through without first considering the consequences.

"I know what we should do" Toluquit said. "Let's go inside and lie down." She immediately agreed it was an excellent idea. This had become a ritual of theirs during their adolescent years when one or both were particularly anxious or sad or both. The daughter would lie next to Toluquit, in his arms. She felt safe when he held her this way. It had been an unusually hot and humid day and both were weary.

They lay down on the daughter's mattress that had been stuffed with Spanish moss, which was commonplace in those days, and to Toluquit, who by then had been sleeping in the corn crib or the out-of-doors for several weeks, it felt heavenly.

No more than an hour had passed when the Wizard arrived back at home. From his pirogue he could not see any sign of activity around the home-site. He poled the boat up onto the mud flat and leaped out without first securing the craft or removing his gear. He rushed to the cabin whereupon he discovered that not only was the stove cool, but there was no food in sight. He then entered the bedroom only to find the couple asleep, cuddled together like babies. The old Wizard could no longer restrain his pent up emotions. Enraged, he began screaming at them, lashing out with his walking stick. Rubbing their eyes in disbelief, they huddled in the corner, where Toluquit used his body to protect the daughter from the Wizard's tirade. This abuse continued unabated until the hysterical shrieks of the daughter so distracted the old man that he finally relented his assault.

The daughter was sobbing uncontrollably as Toluquit tried to calm her. Speaking in French he said, "ça va, il est arrêté et, mon cherie. Y vient à ses sens. (It's alright, my dear. He's stopped and come to his senses, now.) Toluquit dried the daughter's cheeks with the sleeve of his shirt. Then he turned his attention to the Wizard, glaring at him directly in the eye, and delivered a stern warning, "Old man you've lost your privilege. She can no longer stay here in your presence. It is no longer safe for her here. We will leave this dismal place when the Trapper comes again. Muttering a Haitian curse, the old Wizard spit on the floor in front of Toluquit, then turned and walked out.

Toluquit stayed with the daughter until he was satisfied that she was fast asleep. It had been a terrible experience. She had never witnessed such hostility. Once she had settled down she quickly drifted off to sleep. Toluquit lay on his back staring through the spaces in the roof he could see it was a bright, starry, moonless night. He replayed the horrendous event that had unfolded earlier and reckoned that there wouldn't be any more nights like this. He assured himself that his intercession had been appropriate and should have been expected by the Wizard. He vowed that he would begin to make plans for their departure on the Trapper's next visit. He closed his eyes, but sleep did not come easy.

The next morning Toluquit arose, feeling surprisingly refreshed. Sleeping in a bed, even with a lumpy mattress was what his body had badly needed, particularly after the beating he had taken. His back had several bruises, but Toluquit was a very fit young man. His genetic heritage had been very kind and given him an excellently toned physique. And, he was as strong as any mule. Still, soreness was felt in practically every part of his aching body. Even so, he thought, it was still better than a corn crib full of biting vermin.

Toluquit searched for the Wizard but did not find him. The old man went into the swamp almost every day harvesting herbs and wild berries and other useful fauna for his potions and tokens. And, he always had a trotline that needed checking. He was too old now to set out a gator line. Gators were much too big and strong for the old man to handle alone, but his small trotline was good for a couple of catfish or some "sac a' lait" (Cajun French for Crappie or White Perch as they are also known) every week.

It was almost noon before the old man got back to the cabin. He had a bag full of herbs and berries tied to his waist and he had three catfish on a stringer...not a bad day's work for an old man. The Wizard handed the catfish off to Toluquit for cleaning and fileting without so much as a word. Just then the daughter appeared through the cabin's door. At the site of the Wizard approaching she did not advance any further than the front porch.

Slowly climbing the three steps onto the porch the Wizard paused briefly looking her way then continued walking through the opened door into the cabin. The daughter stepped down off the porch and trotted behind Toluquit as he headed to the cleaning board. This was the site where fish, turtles and small game were cleaned and washed. It was nothing more than wide plank of oak secured atop the rail of the small pier jutting out over Petit Bayou Noir (Little Black Bayou). Tied to one side of the pier were a couple of pirogues (dugout canoes) while the other side was always kept open for visitors to tie-up.

Toluquit cut the head off one catfish and tossed it into a large coal bucket, the contents of which were large pieces of inedible meat that were used as bait for the trotline, and the smellier the meat, the better the bait. Cutting through the belly from the gills to the tail he removed the entrails and tossed them into the bayou. Small fish, turtles and crawfish were always nearby and would soon be feeding on these tender morsels.

After the fish were cleaned, Toluquit walked over to where the old man was stirring a fire of red hot coals. He then placed a large black–iron pot filled with lard onto the bed of coals. The daughter dredged the fish filets in corn meal and carefully dropped the pieces into the bubbling grease. Soon she lifted the first batch of fish from the lard then dropped balls of corn-meal, mixed with finely diced wild onions and sugar into the grease. The "hush-puppies" didn't take more than a couple of minutes before turning golden brown at which point she would remove them and put in another batch of fish.

While this second batch of fish cooked the old man placed few pieces of freshly cooked fish onto a tin, pie-pan along with some hush-puppies. He then headed indoors to eat. Before entering the cabin he turned to the couple and asked them to come inside and join him for supper. The couple glanced at one another in dis-belief, but then agreed they would join him.

When they were finished with their food, the Wizard walked over to an old pie-safe and opened the cabinet retrieving a brown jug containing a home brew of corn liquor. It was something the old man always had on hand. He didn't drink openly every day, but on special occasions he would indulge in a couple of shot-glasses of this tonic. He filled the glass to its brim, then, carefully raising it to his lips avoiding any spillage; he threw back his head and swallowed the contents. A most terrible, grimacing face accompanied this act along with a shaking of his head and a loud, "Woo!" To which followed by a broad grin and accompanied by an exclamation, "Mais, dat's strong enuff to knock a Buzzard off a shit wagon, yeah!"

He then poured another shot and offered it to Toluquit. As bad as he did not want to accept it he knew it would be in bad taste (no pun intended) to decline. Toluquit's hand shook visibly as the glass approached his lips, but with closed eyes and a deep breath, he swallowed the drink whole. He'd just as soon have taken a sip from the old coal bucket with the rotting fish heads. The urge to heave was strong as his gut immediately reacted as the liquor reached bottom, followed by a sharp cramping of his stomach muscles. The old Wizard laughed, proclaiming, "It gets you right in da' gut don't it?" Toluquit, smiled sheepishly at the Wizard and nodded in agreement. He dared not respond, knowing very well that opening his mouth would issue forth a torrent of partially digested catfish.

Moments later he excused himself knowing that the rumbling in his gut could no longer be contained.. Rushing outside, he barely reached the water's edge before heaving the contents of his belly into the bayou. Imagining not even the crawfish and minnows would dare taste of it. After a minute or so he assured himself that he had successfully discharged all of the contents of his digestive tract he reentered the cabin, whereupon the old man let out a raucous roar. "It takes a while gettin' use to, no?" Toluquit reckoned that he wouldn't live that long. "Yeah, like never", he replied. The old Wizard let out another roar of laughter, adding. "You make a good point, boy."

Toluquit sat on the weathered bench next to the daughter as the Wizard became quite talkative, animated and openly engaging the young couple in conversation...asking about their day and when they thought the Trapper might be paying them a visit. He then announced that he was going to need them both to assist him in setting some new trotlines. He said since Toluquit was here he might as well help him in hooking some gators. He explained how the gators would provide food, articles of clothing, and money. And, he added, they would all share in the bounty.

Toluquit and the daughter looked at one another and shrugged their shoulders in agreement. Toluquit thought it sounded reasonable enough, but why the sudden change of heart. What were his motivations? He'd go along with the Wizard's plan, but he didn't trust the old Wizard at all. The Wizard told them he would have the pirogues ready for the trip in the morning. After that, everyone went to bed. Even Toluquit, who was once again welcomed to sleep on his pallet on the front porch, where he had been taking his rest prior to his banishment in the corn-crib,

Surprisingly, and in spite of the meal and the after supper drink he enjoyed another good night's rest as well. The next day found the Wizard busy stocking the two pirogues with gear for their trip. He even asked the daughter to fry some cornbread and include some of her blueberry jam which they would take along with them. After everything was in the pirogues and the Wizard had gone over his check list, they shoved off with the Wizard in the lead pirogue and the young couple following behind. It was a mild temperature with little to no humidity, thus providing a great atmosphere for a day's outing.

It was a reprieve from the cramped cabin, a day to enjoy nature and all its beauty. The daughter had brought along some blankets in case of cold weather, but since that was not a factor she decided to make a soft place for her to sit and relax in comfort.

Off in the distance she could see a pair of Bald Eagles tending to their young. She chuckled to herself as she mused, Bald Eagles in a Bald Cypress, very fitting. She watched as otters, in the distance, frolicked in the water. And, beyond the otters she saw an osprey snatch a fish from the water. Over on a mud-bank a big boar coon was busy washing some food. Dragonflies darted about just above the water's surface gliding towards a cluster of Lilly pads. She was certain a fat ol' frog was lying in wait over there for one of them to light close enough to be snatched up with his long, sticky tongue.

Further up was a gator nudging turtles off a partially submerged log that in all likelihood was his favorite place to lie in the morning sun. It seemed that all of nature had come out to welcome them as her eyes feasted on sight after sight. Up ahead of them she watched the Wizard paddle his pirogue with smooth, fluid strokes, barely causing a ripple in the water. He had said before leaving that it would take about an hour to get to the site where he was going to setup the new trotlines. Toluquit had queried why so far away from the cabin to which the Wizard had answered, "Mais dat's where we gonna find da' big gators, fo' shur." It seemed a reasonable answer so he dropped the matter. Now they were off on this excursion and everyone seemed reasonably content, particularly the daughter. She would enjoy the hour's trip in the solitude of nature that was unfolding before them. She could not have imagined the horrors to which the old man's unbridled jealousy would take her and Toluquit.

The next day found the Wizard seated outside his cabin repairing some crawfish baskets for the coming crawfish season. It would be starting next month and he wanted everything to be ready well in advance. He loved trapping deep water crawfish. Suddenly, he heard some racket off in the distance and he dropped his chores and went to see who might be coming his way. In the distance he saw a large flatboat. Several men and a couple of horses could be seen on board. Drawing closer the old Trapper shouted out a greeting in French to which the Wizard did not bother to reply. The pole men nudged the flatboat into the soft mud along the bank near to where the pier was.

The Trapper was the first to disembark, stepping off onto a grassy knoll where his men then secured the flatboat parallel to the mud-bank for the rest of the party and their animals to disembark. The group consisted of two ponies and the two Choctaw Indians that were constant companions of the Trapper particularly accompanying him in the wild. Also along on this trip were two Cajuns, neither of whom spoke any English and whom the Wizard did not know? The Trapper found the old Wizard in a state of terrible distress.

Furiously rubbing his hands together, he stammered and stuttered his way through a dialog that related the happenings of the past couple of days. From what the Trapper could surmise, it seemed that the young couple had grown increasingly difficult to live with. The Wizard conveyed how they were chaffing at having to stay there with him any longer.

They missed their home in the city and they had begged him to take them to the daughter's father, which he had said he could not do. He had explained how the Trapper would be along any day, and when he got here they would all sit down and talk the matter through. But they would have none of that. They insisted that he give them leave, but again he reminded them that their care and well-being were his concern and he would be held responsible. Therefore, he could not allow adolescent reasoning to dictate their actions which would certainly place them in harm's way, because they had no knowledge of the swamp and the dangers that lurked therein.

But they persisted. He pleaded with them to stay through the evening meal and to sleep on it. Then, in the morning, they would discuss the matter again. They were hesitant, but finally relented and agreed to that proposal. In retrospect he could now see that they were already plotting their leave. They were just waiting for the right opportunity. When he had awakened yesterday, he found them gone. They took all their belongings and a pirogue and set off.

He had immediately loaded the remaining pirogue with provisions and set off to search for them, but had soon realized how pointless a search would be as he had no idea in what direction they might have headed? He covered the immediate area of the swamp up to a mile all 'round his home place, but found no evidence of their having traveled that way. The whole day he had called out to them, 'til his voice gave out, but he received no reply. He had been at his wits-end not knowing what to do. He reasoned that if they didn't return by this morning, which was his hope, then he would go into the city and solicit the Trapper's assistance.

The more the old Wizard spoke the calmer his voice became, and the fidgeting of his hands ceased as well. In restoring his composure he also lost any sense of anxiety or concern that he had exhibited when he first began to recount the past couple of days happenings.

The Trapper sensed the Wizard was lying and asked permission for him and his men to thoroughly search the cabin and its immediate surroundings, to which the Wizard readily agreed. It took roughly a half an hour to accomplish the search but nothing belonging to the couple was found, except for something one of the Choctaw's had found and its finding was very telling to anyone knowing the story behind it. What the Indian had found was a small handmade doll, worn threadbare by years of handling. "What is that?" snapped the old Wizard. The Trapper turned to show him what it was they had found. "Oh that! That's nothing... that's just an old ragdoll that was given me by a freeman in Congo Square a while back. It was to be used as a Voodoo doll, but he never paid me, so I just kept the doll."

Unbeknownst to the old Wizard, he had unwittingly stepped into a trap of his own doing, a trap from which he would never escape. Placing the doll securely in the breast pocket inside of his coat, the Trapper then asked the Wizard to tell him more of the doll. The Wizard said, "There's nothing more to tell. It's been misplaced for some time now. Where was it found? May I have it back? It's nothing to you and I can make use of it someday. No, I think not." replied the Trapper. "I'll just hang on to it. Humph!" the old Wizard scoffed. "Suit yourself" he replied, making a wave-off gesture as though it was nothing of concern. The Wizard turned to walk away, but was stopped dead in his tracks by the Trapper's next words.

"This insignificant ragdoll is here to convict you...to testify against you and your account of what befell the young couple placed in your care." Spinning around, the Wizard snapped back angrily, "What's that you say? How can a piece of old, cloth testify against me? I will not stand here while you make wild accusations about me! I have not made an accusation of you as yet." rebutted the Trapper. "But I will accuse you of lying about this doll, for I have known of its existence for 20-years now." The Wizard glared at the Trapper as he continued. "This doll belonged to "Calixte" (Creole name meaning "most beautiful", pronounced: kah-LEEX-tah, and, "Cal" or "Callie" for short). "Who?" boomed the Wizard? To which the Trapper retorted, "Cah-Leex-tah! Cah-Leex-tah!" you don't even know who that is, do you?" But before the Wizard could respond the Trapper continued,

"Calixte is the name of the girl you were entrusted to care for. And this ragdoll that I hold in my hand was her most precious possession. It was a gift from her dearly departed mother and she would never have left this doll behind, old man. Bah!" said the Wizard, "You're just trying to make me confess to something that wasn't my fault! Really?" said the Trapper, "You use words such as, 'accusations, confess' and 'fault' where I have laid neither accusation or blame for anything...until now!" exclaimed the Trapper.

Sensing that the tide was rising against him, the Wizard began to back away towards the cabin. "Old man, what have you done? Where is the couple you have been host to? What have you done to them? Tell me, tell me NOW!" shouted the enraged Trapper. With those words the Wizard turned and bolted toward the cabin securing the door behind him tightly before arming himself with an old scatter-gun and a Colt Dragoon revolver. Darkness was beginning to fall and the men lit torches and staked them at various intervals around the cabin. The Trapper sent the two Choctaws to guard the rear of the cabin while he and the other men were stationed in front.

He next called out to the old Wizard. "Old man, come out unarmed and of your own account and I will see that no harm befalls you." The old Wizard let loose with a volley from his shotgun which blew the front door off its hinges and landed it on the porch. "If you persist to fire upon us I will be forced to burn you out. Come and get me, you Sonova*bitch*! I'll give you a belly full of lead. Don't force me Old man. You cannot win this hand. Give yourself up and I'll guarantee you a fair investigation and trial. You're in no position to make such terms."

shouted the Wizard. "I'll come out when all of you are lying face down in the dirt...dead!

Alright then...have it your way." replied the Trapper. Still, he waited before taking action, but after a quarter-hour had passed, it was obvious what the old Wizard's intentions were. The Trapper gave word to torch the cabin on his command. The Indians had already poured coal oil all around the rear of the building in anticipation of burning the old man out. They would set the rear of the cabin ablaze, with the idea being to drive the Wizard out the front. "OK, old man, this is your last chance. After this...no mercy will be given. Here's my reply you bastard!" said the Wizard and with that he began shooting randomly in all directions with the Colt revolver. "C'mon in you no good piece of shit trapper. I wanna look you in the eye when you die"

With that reply, the Trapper ordered the cabin burned. The Choctaws lit the coal oil and then tossed their torches up on the roof. There was a sudden *whoosh!* from the fire as the coal oil ignited. It wasn't long before the flames engulfed most of the rear of the cabin making it a wall of fire. Since the front door had been blown off by the blast from the Wizard's scatter gun it was an easy target through which several torches were thrown. Minutes later, another volley of shots were fired randomly, to no avail.

Soon, the remainder of the cabin was ablaze, and fiendish laughter was heard, rising and falling in staccato. This laughter soon turned to shrieks of profane cursing... followed shortly thereafter by agonizing screams of suffering and torment that continued until the cabin's ridge pole collapsed. The fire raged for some time consuming the cabin and everything in it, including the old Wizard. Finally, the only sounds to be heard were the crackling of the flames licking the night air. The Trapper ordered that the remaining coal oil be thrown into the fire as it was his intention to eradicate this unholy place and remove any and all signs of its demon resident.

The fire burned most of the night. By morning, the men were sorting through the charred rubble to see if anything remained. All that was found was a blackened foot and nothing more. The Trapp er and his men then searched the swamp for the young couple throughout the remainder of the day. But, by mid-afternoon, not wanting to spend a night in the swamp in the open they decided to abandon their efforts and return to New Orleans to inform the rich Creole of their fateful trip.

The Creole went to the swamp many times with the Trapper and his men searching for a sign, but with each trip it became more apparent that these efforts were in vain and that further excursions would be pointless. Finally, abandoning hope altogether, he lived out his final days in isolation mourning the loss of his lovely daughter and her faithful companion, Toluquit.

His plot to capture the reins of the lucrative Louisiana Sugar and Rice Exchange had been a dismal failure of epic proportions, in the end bringing him nothing but grief. He rarely ventured outside his house except to visit a nearby pipe and tobacco shop. He died a lonely and bitter man largely forgotten by his counterparts. His obituary was a brief line appearing in the business section of the Times Picayune. The once beautiful home fell into decay and was eventually sold at public auction. Today, there is a row of brightly painted shops where once stood this magnificent residence. All that remains of the people who lived there is this story.

EPILOGUE

If you're ever in the vicinity of Congo Square, now Louis Armstrong Park, on a Sunday eve you might hear talk about the old Voodoo Wizard. People still report hearing sinister laughter and bone-chilling screams emanating from the interiors of the swamps, mostly at night. There are those who say that weeping and mournful cries have been heard on moonless nights.

But as this short tale draws to a close, to date not a single sign or piece of evidence of the couple's demise has ever been found. The swamps hold many tales of mysteries and lore and, this is but one. However, in closing, there does remain a brief refrain...written anonymously, it goes something like this:

THE TREE LOVERS-

If ever you're deep in the swamp,

There's a grove of cypress, where the otters romp.

Look to the oak that stands in the bend,

An oak that's home to an old marsh hen.

There you will see what no eyes have seen,

Since that fateful night when the Wizard did scheme.

But look. I say look! Do you see what can't be?

Two faces are trapped 'neath the skin of that tree?

Then you will hear as your thoughts turn to fear.

Turn away, turn away! Do not linger here...

And, do not look back as you flee this site.

For you cannot help them, however you might.

Nor can you bear their mournful pleas.

"Help us, oh help us! Please...won't you, please?"

FINI

THE DEVIL'S AT THE DOOR

A SHORT STORY BY

A. S. West

THE BEGINNING

Nestled on the winding banks of the San Felipe River, 250 miles southwest of Houston, is the community of Hangman, Texas established, more or less, in 1850, back when bands of outlaws and cattle rustlers roamed the countryside. Hangman got its name due to the fact it was the only place within 40 miles of a tree tall enough to hang a man. The country around Hangman was dotted with small arroyos where, if a man were lucky on a hot summer day, he'd find enough water for him and his horse. If only one could drink, it would be the horse as a man alone on foot would have a mighty task before him to walk out of this arid wasteland and into civilization. There were no trees in this part of Texas except for the shrub-like Mesquite and thick patches of Weesatch, which are still in abundance in much of the countryside today, however, neither are sturdy enough to support the weight of a man. But, Hangman had a small grove of Post Oaks and while not towering giants like their big brothers, the mighty live oaks, they were well suited for "stringing a man up." Hangman, in those days, was a thriving community and was the home of the Spotted Owl Cantina which stood in the center of town. The Spotted Owl was a 2-story building with an entrance in the middle with a pair of "batwing" doors. On either side of the entrance were large open shuttered windows. Inside the main hall was a large L-shaped bar that ran the length of the room. Across from the bar was a space containing several tables and chairs. In the back near the staircase to the second floor were three felt covered tables for playing Faro, poker, brag, and three-card Monte. On the second floor were rooms for prostitutes and for overnight travelers.

For a thirsty man with a dry, dusty, throat the Spotted Owl was a veritable Oasis and a haven for cowboys, outlaws, half breed Indians, Villistas, Mexican Banditos, Federales, you name it. On any given night you could find a group in residence. Things really got hot when more than one group crowded around the bar, swilling rot-gut whiskey, warm, foamy beer and home-made Pulque or Mezcal, both capable of causing blindness or one hellava ruckus. Heaven forbid someone was accidentally shot and killed, or worse, purposely shot and sent to his Maker an all-out war could break-out; leaving the Cantina's owner, Jimenez Ortega (Jimmie O), as he was known with unpaid bar bills and dead bodies to dispose of.

Fifty years passed and there was little change except for the colorful characters that rode through town seeking bad whiskey and loose women were long gone. In 1901, there was an occurrence near the town of Beaumont in the southeastern part of the state that would change all of Texas and the entire world. It was there that the Lucas well on Spindletop blew-out, ushering in the Texas oil boom. Nothing was as it was before. In the span of 100 years since that historic occasion most county seats in Texas went from cow-town to multi-faceted, regional trade centers with burgeoning populations. Summers in this region are brutal with daytime temperatures just slightly cooler than the surface of Mercury and when winter arrives, bringing much needed relief from the broiling Texas sun, it is typically mild and too brief. An abundance of wildlife and game are found in the brushy countryside where hunters find excellent opportunities for hunting deer, feral hogs, turkey, quail, doves, and of course Rattlesnakes. Unfortunately for the Quail who nest and lay eggs on the ground and for hunters and biologists alike, Quail populations have be decimated by the invasion of fire ants. Many one-hole towns like Hangman underwent a change for the better. For Hangman there was only one way and that was up, and as the country prospered so did Hangman.

It was to this locale that Billy Ray Hightower found himself one sweltering day in June. Only a matter of a few days had separated

Billy Ray from his arrival in Hangman and the acceptance of a job as a Petroleum Landman with a large, independent firm in Houston. Billy Ray had flown from Nashville, Tennessee, where he and his wife were residing to Dallas, spending an evening with his only daughter. The following day he drove the ten hours from "Big D" to Hangman with a stopover in Houston to meet with Marty Bifford, the president of the company that had hired him. An old friend and a former client of Billy Ray's had made the connection for him to speak to Marty about a position with the company, and within the span of a week of that initial contact Billy Ray was on his way to Texas.

Ten years had lapsed since he had worked the oil fields as a Landman and it had been longer than that since he had stepped inside a courthouse or negotiated an oil and gas lease. For those who do not know what a

Landman is or does, which is practically everyone on the planet, let's take a minute to educate the readers. A Landman by definition is an agent employed by an oil or gas company to secure leases of mineral rights on lands for drilling and/or pooling. These services include, but are not limited to: negotiating for the acquisition or divestiture of mineral rights; negotiating business agreements that provide for the exploration and/or development of minerals; determining ownership in minerals through the research of public and private records; reviewing the status of title, reducing title risk associated with ownership in minerals; managing rights and/or obligations derived from ownership of interests in minerals and more. There is an old adage concerning the advent of oil and gas exploration that says "Nothing can happen until a Landman shows up." And, that's about all there is to say about that.

In the decade of 1975 to 1985, the Hightowers had been a successful team, Billy Ray's wife was an agent in residential real estate, selling several million dollars of upscale housing each year, while, he had established himself as a Landman Broker: by definition, a Landman who has a clientele of oil & gas companies and a stable of independent contractor Landman who work for him to fill the work requirements of his clients. Billy Ray's clientele was composed primarily of small to mid-sized independent oil and gas exploration companies. It's fair to say that the Hightower's lived a comfortable life, not luxurious, but certainly very comfortable.

However, by 1986, the country's economy was in free-fall and it wasn't long before the Hightowers were airborne as well. By 1989, two years after the Savings & Loans / Banking / Real Estate / Oil & Gas Industries tanked, they had reached the end of their rope. In December of that year after losing their home, their vehicles, and most of their hard earned assets, they escaped with little more than the clothes on their backs and some household belongings. Saying goodbye to their Louisiana home of many years, they packed up the kids in a used Subaru that belonged to their daughter who had just finished her freshman year in college, and headed off, looking for a new start and a new life. By the time Billy Ray arrived in Hangman that hot summer day, they had crisscrossed the South reinventing themselves from place to place, but never quite getting their groove back.

HELLO HANGMAN

Upon his arrival in Hangman he checked in with the local office and met briefly with his crew chief and then set out to make suitable lodging arrangements for himself. Typically when a Landman is hired by a Broker, they must pay their own way, including all out-of-pocket expenses, for the first six weeks or so of their employment, which places a heavy burden on the new hiree. The weight of that burden is dependent upon the work requirements, such as an assignment which requires working away from the hiree's home and said hiree's financial stability. In Billy Ray's case, he had barely scraped-up enough money to get to Texas, and he was working out of "right-pocket-bank-and-trust" which indeed was a very short pocket, to say the least.

Having to pay his living expenses for six weeks was going to take a major hat trick even though he had managed to negotiate a weekly advance from his Broker that covered lodging expenses only so Billy figured he'd be living on "Gravy Train and Rolaids" for the first month and from there slowly work his way up to "Kibbles 'n Bits". Billy began the arduous task of searching the Hangman area for affordable, (read cheap) housing and soon discovered to his dismay that the economy in Hangman was thriving, thanks to the surge of drilling activity in the area, and the cost of goods and services, including that of motel accommodations, were way beyond his budget.

Discouraged, yet defiant he was forced to lower his housing standards considerably which meant giving up the normal creature comforts of a more established and recognizable motel chain in lieu of locally owned establishments that might provide him with the basic room and bath at an affordable rate. The search proved a short one as there were no boarding house rooms for rent in the area, and so his search continued a slow descent into what he calls the "cheapo depots" of the "No-tell motels", you know, the ones with the slogan, "If We Had Known You Were Spending the Night, We'd Have Changed the Sheets". Those establishments frequented by hookers, drug addicts and other denizens of the dark searching out illicit profit and/or pleasures, and where the room clerk is ensconced behind 4-inches of bulletproof glass and a drop-box. Trolling the flop houses and other seedy places with rooms for rent was an exhausting ordeal that pretty much took the wind out of Billy's sails. Late in the afternoon with the Texas sun hanging just above the horizon he happened by a tired little motel right on the main highway through town. No doubt he had passed it several times in his search that day, but it had remained undetected until now.

Now, desperate to obtain a place to lay his head after a long and most tiring day he settled into the squalid little motel called "The Americana Inn" located on a wedge of land sandwiched between the railroad tracks and the main Highway, the busiest street in town. By standards set by its competition, The Americana Inn was a veritable 5-star institution that even included a walk-in lobby, rare for most motels in this class which have a walk-up check-in on the street. He guessed it had probably been built in the seventies as it was typical of most motels of that day, being an L-shaped, 2-story structure with probably no more than 50 to 60 rooms. It was anchored on the street by the office from which the vertical leg of the building extended towards the rear of the property where it then connected to the lateral leg by way of a breezeway.

Tucked into the area between the two was the parking lot, an awful, pock-marked piece of pavement capable of accommodating 70 to 80 vehicles, but at this late hour only had a handful of worn trucks and older model cars. The open side of the parking lot was bounded by a chain-link fence which ran parallel alongside the railroad tracks that bisected town.

CHECKING IN TO "LITTLE MEXICO"

The Americana Inn's primary assets were cheap rates, close proximity to his office, and a door with a formidable deadbolt lock. While this establishment met his financial requirements, it just barely met the lowest possible standards by which most people select a place to sleep, that being, cleanliness, safety and comfort. Why it was called The Americana Inn was bewildering except that it was located in America? The Latin Inn would have been far more appropriate, because as he soon learned, he was the only Anglo in residence. Fully half or more of the guests were on long-term rentals and were working for geophysical companies on seismic crews that were busy in this region of Texas at the time. None of these men had vehicles which accounted for the low density parking lot. These hardy individuals worked 12-back-breaking hours a day, 6 days a week, beginning each day at 5:00AM. Most were short, dark and muscular and spoke little if any English. Their days in the field in the south Texas heat were spent clearing land, running cables and digging shot-holes.

 In the evenings they would gather in small groups outside their rooms drinking beer and grilling meat they had purchased at the nearby H-E-B supermarket. The thick smoke from their black iron grills drifted across the parking lot, permeating every room with the smell of Mesquite. Billy envied these men, certainly not because of their work, but because of the camaraderie they obviously enjoyed. It was obvious they relished this time of day when they could refresh themselves from the rigors of their long days in the field and enjoy one another's company, drinking and sharing the evening meal. After supper when the grills had been put away most retired to their rooms to watch TV, some lingered awhile outside engaging in after dinner conversation and a last cigarette before retiring for the evening. By eight o'clock everyone was tucked into bed and lights out. The parking lot which an hour earlier had bristled with life was now empty. At 8:01PM, you could hear a cricket fart two-blocks away.

By comparison, it could be said Billy Ray, slept the morning away as his typical workday began at 8:00am and ended between 5 and 6pm. By the time he arrived back at the motel or, "Little Mexico", as he now referred to it, the evening fiesta was in full swing in the "Town Square" aka, the parking lot, replete with ear-drum piercing Mariachi music blaring from a couple of behemoth speakers that were rolled out whenever the men were in residence.

Walking from his car to his room, particularly that first week as a resident, he felt like the white guy on the "Jeffersons" TV show, and he could feel all eyes following his every step. Billy still hadn't cleared his first pay-check but he was working on an advance that at the least permitted him to buy decent food and not just snacks. It had become a part of the evening ritual after work to grab a bag of burgers and fries or some fried chicken and return to his room to relax and enjoy his food. He coveted the waiting coolness of his room and the opportunity to retreat from the stifling heat. This would be the first time during a hectic day when he could relax. Once inside the room he would immediately turn down the A/C, strip off his sweaty clothes down to his skivvies, and pour himself a large drink of cola over ice. Then, perching, cross-legged on the end of the bed, bag of food in his lap, he watched the evening news while eating his meal. After supper, he would watch TV for an hour or so before finally drifting off to sleep. And so it went day after day, week after week.

SATURDAY NIGHTS FEVER

Saturday nights, usually beginning around 6:00PM, the "pavement princesses" or hookers began to appear. These "working girls" plied their trade among the Mexican residents who by now had received their weekly pay, always in cash. The first few weekends I watched these women with some fascination as they would approach a group of men, and begin to flirt and dance very seductively for them. They would watch attentively for a time, but soon a man would stand up and offer his hand to a woman. She would take his hand and the two of them would disappear into a room.

Shortly, they would reappear and another man might offer his hand. On rare occasion, a woman might reject a man's hand and this would lead to an argument with other me heckling the rejected man. There were times men competed with each other for the attention of a woman, yet still at other times a group of men might rebuff a women's seducing enticements shooing her away with the backs of their hands. The girls repeated this until they had worked all the available "Johns" for that night.

During this time the fiesta continued unabated with lots of beer drinking and Tequila shots, and always the steady blare of Latino and Mariachi music that seemed to increase several decibels with each passing hour. This reverie would continue throughout the late night and into the early morning hours punctuated with periodic crescendos of deafening music loud enough to vibrate the glass windows in the fronts of the motel's rooms and usually laced with hysterical cries of "Hi-Yee" and accompanied with outbursts of drunken laughter.

Over time Billy Ray paid little attention to these goings-on, but for the first few weekends he joined in the festivities as a spectator only sitting outside his room drinking beer and watching the pageantry of lively, albeit, crude entertainment. With time, however he merely went through his daily routine, becoming oblivious to his surroundings, blotting out the people, the place and all of its activity. And, the residents, also having grown accustomed to seeing him on a daily basis paid him little attention as well.

THE DAILY GRIND

Every morning Billy exited the motel parking lot around 7:30 onto the busy street that ran along the frontage. It was a five minute drive to the office if he didn't catch a train, and then after a half-hour or so in the office attending to paperwork and whatnot, he would be out in the field the remainder of the day. At the end of each day's work, he continued the habit of stopping to purchase food and groceries. He did not fraternize with the rest of his work crew because his finances did not permit any sort social life outside of working and the occasional lunch with workmates. It was just as well because by the end of the day he was simply too tired, having spent a long day in the heat.

Most of his driving in the field consisted of short hops lasting 5 to 10 minutes. That way he would be out of the car talking to landowners in the outdoors, owners in the outdoors, then back in the car where the heat index had risen to a temperature sufficient to pop popcorn. With the A/C blowing full blast he would just be reaching a point of cool down when he would arrive at his next stop and, back out into the open again. After a couple of months on the job this hectic routine abated for the most part as he had learned his way around the countryside and the best time to visit or call on the local landowners. Other days he ran records in the courthouse or searched the tax assessor's office...on these days he was indoors most of the day and he realized that he needed those days desperately because it was now August and the combination of extreme, humid heat was almost unbearable. He could not imagine working under the conditions of the fellow

Americana Inn residents. There had to be something in their DNA that permitted them to work and survive in such heat.

As mentioned previously, the first thing he'd do after getting back to the room each evening was to turn down the A/C. The Americana Inn may have been a shit-hole motel, but that air-conditioner alone was worth the price of admission...well, almost?

Thank goodness the room cooled quickly which was important because upon leaving each room the maids always made certain to adjust the thermostat to a setting at which the only way the A/C could possibly cycle on was if the room were to suddenly burst into flames... That way you see, by the time he got back at the end of the day the ambient temperature of the room was slightly cooler than, oh I don't know...say the pavement in the parking lot... but not by much. Two things in which he has always placed a high premium on, good air-conditioning and clean air-conditioning, in that order.

And then there was this smell. Smells have different connotations. That is it can be a pleasant smell or it can be a god-awful smell. This smell, this odor, this reeking, putrid, decomposing corpse sealed in the wall smell had no chance of ever being classified remotely as pleasant. You know how far East is from West? Well this smell is way further than that from good. This smell is something God Almighty has reserved for Satan and his demon hordes. Anyway, this foul stink was particularly noticeable the moment the room's door was ajar. It would billow out the way heat escapes from a blast furnace. It was as if the heat were attempting to escape the rotting awful smell it had been trapped in all day long. Following the initial shocks to the sensory system, he was reminded of the "Motel 6" jokes concerning their other notable slogan, "Yeah, we're working on that smell thing." Billy had purchased a can of room spray at the local H-E-B, only because they didn't sell it in a 50-gallon drum with a foot-pump. The can only lasted a few days, so for now he would just eat and enjoy his meal which always made him feel better. In the end he decided the scent of warm food helped mask the funk better anyway...

After supper He'd fix a tall glass of soda and settle on to the bed usually with a snack of some sort and watch a couple of hours of TV. Meanwhile, outside beyond the heavily bolted door to his room the usual night creatures would be winding down their day as well. Weary but satiated, exhausted, but cool, he would drift off to sleep. Several weeks passed this way without exception.

However, early one morning, he was awakened by loud noises coming from the room above him. From the sounds, somebody seemed to be in distress. He could hear a shrill feminine voice rising then falling above the Baritone voice of a man speaking Spanish, he believed. There were heavy footfalls and the sound of something or someone striking the wall with a loud thump. Then as suddenly as it began, it subsided. All was quiet. He listened for a time before drifting off to sleep again.

A DAY IN THE COUNTRY

Since Billy was staying over on weekends in those days he would try to entertain himself by getting out and doing some local sightseeing. One such Saturday morning, bright and early, he decided to make a day trip to into the surrounding countryside. Some distance away was a sleepy little hamlet named Goliad that is rich in Texas history and situated on the San Antonio River.

On the outskirts of town is The "Presidio Nuestra Señora de Loreto de la Bahía", known more commonly as "Presidio La Bahia", or simply "La Bahia" or "Presidio". It is a fort constructed by the Spanish Army, ca 1749, that became the nucleus for the city of Goliad, so named supposedly an anagram of Hidalgo (I guess they didn't know where to place the "H" so they just said "screw it!" and left it off), in honor of priest Miguel Hidalgo, the father of the Mexican War of Independence. The present day Presidio was rebuilt in 1771 and was captured by insurgents twice during the Mexican War for Independence.

Goliad was also the site of the first offensive action of the Texas Revolution as well as the site of the largest massacre to occur during those violent years. The "Goliad Massacre", as it became known, accounted for twice the loss of life as that at the Alamo, whose fall occurred some months prior.

Goliad is known as "The Birthplace of Texas Ranching" and is the seat of government for Goliad County. Dominant on the town's square is the county courthouse, an imposingly elegant structure of brick and sandstone adorned with five cupolas. Around the square are quaint antique shops, boutiques and cafes along with offices for attorneys and abstractors and a few private residences as well.

Billy enjoyed the leisurely drive and spent the day browsing antique shops, flea markets and other historic sites. Late in the afternoon he enjoyed a hearty Mexican meal of soft chicken and beef Tacos served with refried beans, crispy chips and spicy salsa, washed down with couple of cold Cervezas. One of the great pleasures of working in this part of the country was the abundance of excellent Mexican food which Billy loved with a passion. He enjoyed being able to walk into a restaurant famished and after being seated diving into a basket of freshly cooked corn chips and warm, spicy salsa, and slaking his thirst with an icy, cold beer. It was the perfect end to a perfect day.

His appetite satiated he relaxed, gazing out of the large picture window in the front of the café. The afternoon was fading fast and thin streamers of iridescent clouds glowed in splendor as the sun, now just a golden orb, hung lazily above the horizon in the wide Texas sky. His thoughts drifted back to the times when he used to hunt doves in this country years ago. This time of day would usually find him under the shade of a Mesquite tree, near a tank, gun at the ready, waiting for some doves to come in to drink (Tank: A watering hole, natural or man-made) Billy loved hunting doves, but they are skittish little buggers and can be difficult to knock down. They are capable of aeronautical maneuvers that defy the dynamics of flight. But no matter how speedy they may be or whatever wonders of flight they might be capable of, they all need to drink.

At this time of day when the sun hovered low in the sky, they would begin searching for a watering hole. Doves drink water like horses with their heads down. They are capable of sucking and swallowing, unlike other birds that have to scoop and raise their heads allowing gravity to aid in swallowing. If you happened to be at the right tank, then that is where the playing field got leveled. Later, walking back to the Mule$_3$ (Mule: A small, 4-wheeled, ATV, produced by Kawasaki) pockets full of plump dove breasts, ready for eating that night.

This region of Texas produces an interesting and diverse landscape unlike any other. Interspersed among the gentle rolling hills and bluffs dotted with thick stands of post oaks are long stretches of flat, sandy loam where cattle graze. In other places the land has succumbed to the advance of underbrush and is choked with mesquite a much sought after tree whose wood produces a unique, piquant smoke that many people cherish for BBQs or for grilling and smoking meat. Growing beside and under the Mesquite is a short willowy tree-like shrub that grows like a weed. Unlike Mesquite the Weesatch, a type of Acacia is a nuisance, practically good for nothing except producing cover for a myriad of game such as hogs, turkey, deer, doves and others seeking refuge under its cover. Years ago the flower of the Weesatch was collected to manufacture French perfume in the 19th century, a little known fact to most landowners who curse its existence today.

It was dark by the time Billy got back to the motel and the Saturday night fiesta ritual was in full swing. Entering the parking lot he found it was packed, every parking space was taken. This caused him to have to circle the lot a couple of times in search of a vacant spot. He finally found one about as far from his door as he could get and still be on the Motel's premises. He complained bitterly to himself as he was laden with groceries, and, as he neared the door to his room he discovered there was a vacant parking place directly in front of his door. "What the Hell?" he muttered. It must have opened up after his second pass around the lot. "It figures" he mused.

At the precise moment he reached the door a pair of headlights swept across the room and the rumbling sound of a large truck pulled into the space directly behind him. He had just set the bags down on the walkway to dig into his pockets for his room key. Upon finding it, he slipped the key into the lock and turned the bolt while pushing against the heavy door with his foot. He placed his trashcan in front of the door to hold it open. Picking up his bags of groceries he proceeded straight toward the vanity area placing them on the washbasin's countertop. The headlights from the truck were still on, on high-beam no less, and the light flooded the cramped room like a search light from a gulag or stalag...a prison, you know! Staring at the lights momentarily in the mirror over the sink he wondered just how long Mr. Inconsiderate was going to leave them on.

Billy turned and faced the open door and for a moment he simply stared into the blinding light, thinking the driver would see that gesture and, as a courtesy, would turn off his headlights. No such luck. Then, raising a hand in front of him to shield his eyes he walked slowly to the door. He couldn't see anything beyond the beams except for the outline of a large pick-up; a diesel powered dually no-doubt judging by the engine clatter and the silhouette of the truck itself. With one hand on the door knob and the other still shading his eyes, he mumbled more to himself than the driver, "I hope can you see alright, Shithead!"

Before the door closed a voice called out in a strong Spanish accent, "Whad you say, Gringo? Nothing, Nada", Billy answered, closing the door and rolling the bolt on the lock. Before Billy could turn around there was a knock on the door. "Oh shit!" Billy sighed, this could only be trouble. "Hey, Buddy! I wanna talk wit'chu! Open dis fuckin' door!" Then a female voice said something to the man, which was followed by a loud thump at the door as he kicked it.

"Joto! Maricón! Besa mi culo, puto!" He shouted, before walking away. Now, Billy knew just enough Spanish to get him into a bar fight with any Tejano possessing the testosterone of a pissant, and knew this guy was not inviting him to come out and play with him and his friends. "Oh, Hell No! Bite Me!", He murmured. Billy grabbed a cold beer and a bag of Doritos and flopped onto the lumpy bed, fluffing the pillows. When he was comfortable he grabbed the remote and turned on the TV, scanning the channels for something that would distract him from this evening's brief interlude with Mr. Macho-Man... All these weeks he had been the only gringo in the motel and not one incident. Hell, he hadn't made a ripple in the water since checking in. And that's just the way he wanted it to be to be seen, but not seen; someone who goes unnoticed, someone who fades into the background. And, he'd been very successful at doing just that. That is until tonight. He hadn't started anything, he rationalized; it was the frickin' truck driver who started this shit. "Son-ova-bitch!"

Later on, he got up to grab another beer and on his way back to the bed. "*wham!*" There was a sudden kick at the door. He almost pissed his pants. He was totally not expecting that. "Oh, shit! The Macho-Bastard was back". "Hey, Gringo! You in there, man? (Chuckling) I hope I didn't wake you, man! C'mon, man, open de door." Again He hears a female voice calling to him in a pleading tone. "Shut-Up, Bitch! I not talking to you. Get inna fucking truck?" Then another kick at the door followed by a hail of expletives in Spanish that trailed off as he climbed into the cab of his monster-truck and turned the key. "*vroom-vroom!*" roared the truck. Then the high-beam lights were on again, a beam of light like the tracker-beam from the Empire's Death Star shone through the worn curtains of his window filling the room with bright light, once again! Billy dared not make a move toward the bed knowing the Mexican would certainly see him and it would probably provoke him further. Billy heard him yell out of the truck's window as he drove off, "Duerma tranquilo, Maricon!" Followed by the roar of the big engine as he rumbled out of the parking lot onto Highway in front of the motel...then, burning rubber, as he sped off into the night.

Oh, screw this guy, Billy thought, as he lay in bed staring at the ceiling. Billy wondered what new bung-hole motel he'd be staying in tomorrow night? This son-ova-bitch has completely screwed-up my life. He chugged the rest of his beer and hit the light switch on the bed-stand. The colored lights of the motel's neon sign shone brightly on the wall opposite his bed filtered by the flimsy curtains.

Staring at the muted colors, his thoughts flitting about like a house-fly in a hot room. It had been a long day and his lumpy bed was a comfort to his weary bones. For now he'd forget about the Mexican. It wasn't long before Billy was asleep. The next morning as he awoke, he lay there in bed gathering his thoughts. It seemed as though last night's confrontation was more like a dream than reality. His thoughts retraced the events replaying them un his mind. His recall was vivid. Nope, it was real, alright. Well, if this ain't a shitty way to get up in the morning I don't know what is, he cussed? He rolled out of bed and padded to the bathroom.

A VISIT WITH JORGE

Closing the room door behind him Billy noticed that the parking lot was practically empty save for an old rusted-out, flat-bed truck parked against the chain-link fence that looked as though it had been there forever. However, just down from his room was a cherry '77 Coup De Ville Lowrider with custom fleck red-paint job and enough chrome to set off a TSA metal detector on a drive-by. Billy stopped momentarily to admire the ride. Bajito y suavecito, the Chicanos called it: low and slow. He wondered if this bad-boy could still hop? Must belong to a one-nighter, he deduced. Then, surveying the empty lot again he wondered, "Where the hell is everyone?" It looked like it does after an INS raid. He decided whatever it was it didn't concern him. "*Hmph!*", he snorted, and continued his walk to the office. Usually on Sunday mornings things are a little laid back. NO! Check that. They're a lot laid back. The Seismic crews don't work Sundays so, some of the men would be sleeping in. Others just hung out, loitering around the parking lot or drifting from room to room for conversation, still others attended Mass at the Catholic Church of Guadalupe, a couple of blocks over. Most Sunday afternoons the men would walk in groups to the Walmart or the nearest H-E-B store both some distance away. There they could spend some leisure time browsing the aisles for personal supplies and such. Today was different. Billy couldn't not put his finger on it but it just felt different, something wasn't right? But, since he couldn't determine whether that was a good thing or a bad thing, he just shrugged it off as an anomaly.

The bells above the door clanged as Billy entered the small, dank room. A shaft of light emitted from a tiny window above the door was the only light save for a crooked, goose-neck lamp on the desk that sat behind and below the check-in counter. A small cloud hovered just above the countertop, fed by a steady column of smoke from the cigar clenched in the corner of Jorge's mouth. As always, he was seated at his desk, with a half cup of coffee, several partially eaten doughnuts and an ashtray that hadn't been emptied in 3-years. Newspapers were scattered about the desk and onto the floor. The sports section of the Houston Chronicle was folded and had red marks and notes scribbled on several pages. Jorge looked up at Billy through his bloated, red eyes, his thick reading glasses perched on the end of his nose. Beneath that bulbous schnoz was a moustache that Pancho Villa would have killed for. Wedged in the corner of his mouth and resting on a bottom lip that was as wide as a running board on a Model A Ford was a fat Churchill cigar that probably cost a quarter. It was burned half-way down. It was always burned just half-way down. It was as if Jorge had this incredible supply of "half-smoked" cigars. Maybe he bought 'em that way? Jorge bounced out of his chair like ICE had just appeared. "Mee-ster Hightower, how are you today, it's good to see you. You are looking well? His voice rising giving the impression it was more a question than an observation... Are your accommodations acceptable? Are the maids cleaning your room properly? What brings you here so early on a Sunday morning? (signing himself as he continued to speak) Is there something I can do for you today? What? What is it that you need? Tell me? Well, for starters, Jorge you could just shut the fuck-up, for a second!" Billy answered. With that, Jorge liked to bust a gut he laughed so hard. "Mee-ster Hightower, you are a funny man, a very funny man. OK, I'll be quiet now. Why did you come here this morning?

Jorge", Billy paused to make sure Jorge was paying attention and to convey to him that what he was about to say was of some importance. "Jorge" Billy repeated. "What do you know about a Mexican that drives a big black truck, a Ford F-350, I'm guessing, tricked out, maybe a King Ranch or Eddie Bauer edition, you know, double cab, big, knobby tires, custom lighting on top and underneath?" Jorge got very serious. He glanced both ways as if to ensure no one could hear what he was about to say. Then, the unbelievable happened....He took the cigar out of his mouth. Holy Shit and Good Night Nurse! This must be apocalyptic, Billy thought to himself. Leaning forward he began to speak. "*Ooohhh*, Mee-ster Hightower, hees a very baaad man. He is not someone you would want to be associated with. Yeah, Jorge, I got that feeling last night. He didn't exactly roll out the red carpet for me. You saw heem last night?" Jorge's voice rising once again, as he spoke. "Well, in a manner of speaking, more like he saw me, but that doesn't matter. What else can you tell me about him?" Jorge swallows hard and replaces the wet end of his cigar deep in the corner of his mouth, rolling it several times with his tongue before speaking. "OK, his name is Antonio Rialto Domingues, but he's known by everybody as 'Dom Diablo', you know, the Devil? Yeah I know, Jorge" Billy answered stoically. "So, what, he runs girls, obviously? What else? Dope? Guns? Is he a Coyote? (a man who Runs illegals across the border?) To each question Billy posed,

Jorge responded, "Si-Si Alright then" Billy announced, "So, he's not a candidate for The Rotary Club's 'Citizen of the Year'."

"I've never seen him before last night, what's the deal with that?" Jorge responded saying, "He has a schedule. He works different towns on different days or weeks. He comes to Hangman once a month, usually for two nights. Then, he's gone 'til the next month. Last night was his first night so he's sure to come back tonight. Mee-ster, Hightower, you need to leave.... Right NOW! You don't want to be here when he comes back. Excellent idea, Jorge; except for one problem what's that, Mee-ster Hightower?" Jorge said, blinking his big eyes several times in wonderment. "I've got nowhere to go. You know the old saying, you can run, but you can't hide? Of course...?" Billy paused as if to consider a point before continuing... "*Hmmm*, I could always stay here with you, Jorge. Here in your quarters. Oh, Mee-ster, Hightower, I, I" Before he stuttered another syllable Billy let him in on the joke. "I'm just kidding, Jorge. I wouldn't do that to you." The fat man let out a long breath of air tainted with coffee and stale cigar, like a balloon suddenly deflating, as if he had held his breath while Billy made his proposal. Then, upon hearing Billy's confession, he relaxed and allowed himself to breathe again. Aware of his overture and embarrassed by it, Jorge grinned sheepishly and blinked his big eyes once again, nodding his head, "Yes-yes!" as if listening intently for Billy's next remark. "Besides, Jorge, Dom Diablo would have little trouble finding me if he wanted to. No, Jorge. I'm gonna stay right here... in your motel, that is." Again Jorge let out a sigh of relief followed by a sheepish grin. Billy then continues, "I figure he was on a rant last night. He's probably slept it off by now. No-no, Mee-ster Hightower!" Jorge interjected, fully regaining composure. "Dom D', he don't sleep nuthin' off once he makes up his mind about som-teen. No, you must leave. You need to go. Go Now!" Jorge insisted. "Well I'm gonna do just that! Good!" replied Jorge, "I'll get your bill ready." Billy laughed, "Not so fast my friend, I meant I was gonna go run a few errands before heading back to my room to get some rest. One thing's for certain, if 'Dom D' should show up it'll probably be after 8:00pm when everyone's gone to bed. That gives me some time to rest up and figure out what kinda' reception I can arrange for him should he decide to pay me a visit, but first things first. Right now I'm gonna go to the 'Country Bakery' for a bag of Kolaches and some Tea Cakes. Man, they make Tea Cakes almost as good as my wife's little granny used to make 'em. Damn! I'm hungry just thinking about 'em. Can I get you something, Jorge? No, Meester Hightower, Gracious, mucho gracious." Jorge answered. The little bells jangled as Billy walked out of the office into the bright sunlight. Replacing his sunglasses, Billy eyes quickly scanned the area. Satisfied with what he saw, he decided to walk the short distance to the bakery. He always felt rejuvenated after a brisk walk and it helped to clear his mind for more serious thought than Kolaches and tea cakes

A CHANCE ENCOUNTER?

Two weeks passed and Billy's daily grind remained unchanged. Nothing remarkable or memorable occurred and he was beginning to think that Dom Diablo had changed his schedule or his mind, deciding Billy wasn't worth the effort. In any event Billy was feeling pretty comfortable with the fact that he wouldn't see Dom again. Then one Saturday afternoon he was in his room doing some paperwork. He got up to fix a drink and realized he was out of ice. Picking up the ice bucket he headed toward the ice machine, located in the breezeway a couple of doors down.

Just as he swung open the door to his room open, a Chicano clutching the arm of a pretty, young woman nearly collided with him. "Pardon!" Billy apologized for his infraction. The man simply glared at him, but the young girl smiled beguilingly at Billy before lowering her gaze. Her companion, aware of the gesture, suddenly jerked her arm as a reminder and she quickly looked away. Billy watched as the couple walked down the sidewalk towards the rear of the building. He was a short, muscular Mexican with shoulder length hair. He was wearing a black t-shirt, starched Wrangler jeans and a pair of black, full-quill Ostrich boots. The girl was a slim, Tejano in her late teens or early 20's. Her dark, brown hair was pulled back in a yellow ribbon. She wore a bright blue, cotton blouse and a short matching skirt which accentuated her long, tanned legs.

The couple stopped at the last door, knocking softly 3 or 4 times. Then the male whispered into the girl's ear; his eyes nervously searching the area around him as he waited for the door to open. He glanced back up the walk in Billy's direction, not looking at him so much as looking past or through him. The girl looked forlorn glancing briefly Billy's way as the door opened. The male said something to the person inside the room. He then nodded his head and pushed the girl inside. The door slammed behind them. Billy was still standing in front of the open door of his room, watching and thinking to himself, "This guy must be one of Dom's guys?" Suddenly, Billy was aware of his inquisitive posture and immediately shook-off the lapse in concentration.

Then, placing a trash can in the door jamb to keep the door open so he wouldn't have to fumble for his room key on his return, Billy then ambled casually down the sidewalk and around the corner through the open breezeway to the ice machine. As he filled the bucket with ice, he became aware of the tenseness in his stomach muscles. He mulled the events over in his mind and wondered if this had simply been a chance occurrence or was it perhaps a hint or a portent of things to come. Reaching his room and seeing the partially open door served to remind him that he couldn't be so careless in the future. He needed to keep his guard up and be on the alert to the fact that Dom was still out there. Maybe he hadn't gone away at all. Maybe he was waiting for Billy to let down his guard.

Awhile later, Billy went to his car to retrieve his briefcase. His car was parked on the second row away from his room. As he closed his car door he glancing in the direction of where he last saw the couple. The Mexican was now walking back up the sidewalk alone. Around his neck was a heavy gold chain holding a large cross that swung back and forth across his chest as he walked and the clatter of his cowboy-heeled boots grew louder with each step. A chill ran up Billy's spine and he felt that discernible knot again in his gut. The Mexican gazed at Billy with dark, brooding eyes. Billy noticed he clutched a pair of sunglasses in one hand and he thought it unusual that on a bright, sunny day, he wasn't wearing his glasses? Maybe he wanted Billy to see he was staring at him? His heavy brow and dark eyes were pinched together and His footsteps seemed deliberate as he closed the distance between himself and Billy.

Billy's first instinct was to hurry his own steps. But, he resisted that urge as he did not want to give away his uneasiness. Composing himself he turned his attention to giving an air of indifference, hoping to convey the notion that the Mexican's presence and gaze was of no concern to him. Arriving at his door Billy inserted the key. For a moment he considered speaking to the Mexican as they were now only a few feet apart. But Billy quickly rejected the idea and instead simply ignored the man. Closing the door behind him he noticed the noisy boot clatter had ceased. Billy leaned against the door, listening intently. Not a sound. Then, as Billy stepped away from the door he heard the sound once again. Billy continued to listen until he could no longer hear the noise. He waited a moment or two then opened the door to survey the sidewalk and parking lot for any sign of the Mexican. Satisfied he was gone Billy re-entered his room, closing and bolting the door behind him. So, the man had stopped at Billy's door. Interesting, Billy thought. Dom, if all this did involve him, seemed to be playing a game of cat and mouse with Billy.

From that moment forward Billy vowed never to be unprepared. It would seem apparent that Dom hadn't forgotten the incident that had brought them together. Jorge was right about Dom forgiving and forgetting. Billy acknowledged, that the practice of leaving access to his room while he was out of it even for a moment was something he could not permit to happen again. There was a weak link in that chain of thought and that was there were always a few moments while unlocking his door when he was exposed to threat. Over the next few days, Billy practiced unlocking and closing his door. And, in doing that exercise he realized that the real threat came when he was inside his room, yet the door had not fully closed fully behind him. So, he then practiced that until he was satisfied that his chances of surprise attack were greatly diminished.

Days later, Billy realized that the wait for Dom's next move was beginning to wear on him. He was getting paranoid, seeing practically every Hispanic as a possible threat. He needed to control his thoughts, but how? This anxiety was interfering with his sleep as well. A month had passed since the encounter with the Mexican and Billy thought that if Dom was truly after him it would happen on his next visit to Hangman. On a particularly restless night Billy was halfway through one of his all-time favorite movies, "The Man Who Shot Liberty Valance" When he suddenly picked up the remote, killing the TV. He then rolled onto his right side and turned off the bedside lamp.

Lying there in the still twilight of the room he contemplated what events might be spiraling headlong towards him. Staring at the ceiling his eyes adjusted to the eerie yellow glow that illuminated the room. Jorge had installed some stadium-type, million-watt lighting system in the parking lot to prevent vehicle break-ins or other crimes. These lights not only lit up the parking lot and everything in it but also permeated all the rooms that faced the lot as well. The blackout curtains were old and worn and were not very effective. In addition to that they didn't fully close. Therefore, light easily shined through these gaps in the blackout curtains, thus creating a beam of yellow light that cascaded across the bed and onto the opposite wall,. Like everything else that was wrong in this little slice of paradise in which he now lived, Billy had grown accustomed to it and had accepted all its flaws and deficiencies that were so abundantly obvious throughout Jorge's Americana Inn.

And even though tonight was not unlike every other night he had spent there he couldn't be lulled to sleep by the light. Now he was on his side which he preferred when sleeping. As he studied the blank wall before him he recalled an old metaphysical blank-wall meditation exercise that he had attempted to use back when he studied all the metaphysical religions and spiritual movements popular during the New Age decade of the '70s. Billy laughed out loud, thinking, well, you've come full circle, Billy-boy. In those days of enlightenment he was like an awful lot of folks that were searching for answers. Thinking back, he mused, he didn't even have the right questions. What he did discover was that all those systems only left a person with a lot more questions than answers. However, this exercise might have some merit tonight, after all, meditation serves to empty one's mind of clutter, the purpose being to achieve a deeper consciousness or maybe it was a higher consciousness or awareness, who the hell knows?

Anyway, it was a practice he had found to be useless, but tonight it seemed to help him empty his mind of distraction and achieve some higher level of focus. He was desperate to distract his mind from any thoughts of fear and failure. Billy then fervently prayed that God would protect and deliver him from the impending evil he felt was coming his way. In any event he would not allow his mind to succumb to the wave of terror that sought to scare him into submission. He would not let that happen. If he were to let this seep into his consciousness he was as good as dead. But, Now he was resolved to fight back no matter what the consequences might be. Eventually Billy closed his eyes. He thought about his family. Lord, how he wished he were with them at this moment. Not them being here with him, but him being there with them. Thinking of them only strengthened his resolve to defeat the powers he felt were coming against him. Oh God, don't let go of me, he cried. Hold on to me!

AN UNEXPECTED CALLER

Several hours of restless sleep passed when suddenly he sat bolt upright in bed, as if his brain had been zapped into awareness with a cattle prod. What the Hell was that? He thought. He cocked his head to one side listening for a sound, any sound. He had often wondered why he did that that is...tilting his head to one side when straining to hear something. He had noticed that dogs will on occasion do the same thing. No matter. He was pretty certain he didn't have any canine genes. In any event, Billy sat there in bed, listening, waiting for the slightest sound. It was unearthly quiet. That should have been a signal that something was amiss. As his eyes adjusted again to the yellow-glow of the room he sensed a presence. As if someone were in the room; someone or something was in his room. He could feel their presence. Now, these days Billie carries a weapon, a Sig P245and with his CCP (Concealed Carry Permit) he is always cocked and locked. But that night in the half-light of room #108, he was unarmed. Billy sat motionless trying not to breathe and listening for the slightest sound. The only thing he was acutely aware of was the beating of his pulse in my ears. It was deafening! As his eyes darted about the room he detected a slight movement, a shadow perhaps. No! There! It moved again. He couldn't make out who or what, but a slender form appeared to be cowering in the corner of his room under the vanity area. Billy caught his breath. Oh my god! Is that an alien?!. It looked like a slender grey humanoid figure. He was wide-eyed and still breathless over what he was looking at. Now he could hear shallow breathing, not his. Then a faint whimper punctuated the stillness. His heart was about to explode through his chest; his pulse throbbed in his neck. "Who's there?" He managed; his voice shaking as he spoke. There was no reply, except for a slight, almost imperceptible whimper that really freaked him out. Was this the only one? There must be more "Who's there, dammit!?" he demanded in a sterner tone, half hoping to bolster his self-confidence and, frighten whomever, whatever was in the room with him. "Please...Senor, I..." came a quivering, half-finished response.

It was the voice of a female. His confidence now partially regained, Billy threw back the bedcovers and swung his legs over the side of the bed while reaching for and turning on the bedside lamp. The sudden shock of light filling the room blinded him momentarily, but his eyes quickly adjusted, and he could see a young Tejano girl crouched in the corner under the vanity. Her long dark hair was matted against the left side of her face and her nose and mouth were bloody. Tears streamed down mascara stained cheeks, and Billy recognized her as the young girl he had seen earlier with the Chicano. For a moment, all they could do was stare at one another. There, motionless in the dimly-lit room, each desperately searching the other's eyes; hers filled with terror, his filled with bewilderment and confusion. The terror in her eyes was as real as the tears that streamed down her cheeks. Her gaze shifted and she stared blankly ahead, a thousand yard stare. the kind of stare that comes over a person when something really awful has happened. It looked as though she was staring at something or someone behind Billy, someone who was in another dimension perhaps, definitely not someone in the room with them... or, maybe it was and he couldn't see it?

Billy slowly approached her. She pulled her knees up under her chin and began to shake. "It's OK", he said softly, trying to reassure her. "I'm not going to hurt you." He squatted in front of her. "Let me help you" He offered, as he reached for her. But she drew further back into the corner under the vanity counter. "Are you hurt badly", he asked? She shook her head slowly from side to side; her eyes still gazing off at some distant horizon. "Look, Billy said, let me help you. Let me call the police. "NO!" she shouted "Please", she pleaded, "No policía! Okay", he said, "But tell me what happened to you. Who did this? A man", she replied, her lips quivering as she spoke the words. "He'll be looking for me", she continued. "He won't leave without me. Was it the guy I saw you with earlier?" She shook her head indicating it was not. "OK", he said.

By now he could see that she had been banged-up pretty badly and appeared to have a lot of blood coming from her nose and mouth. Billy soaked a washcloth with cold water from the ice bucket and offered it to her. She gently pressed it against her mouth and grimaced. A mixture of blood and water trickled down her chin and throat. "Alright, let's get you out from under this sink and have a look at you." Taking hold of her hands Billy helped her to her feet. She was a mess; aside from her bloody countenance, a large edema bulged below her right eye impairing her vision, the eye would soon close. Her makeup was smeared across her face and streaks of mascara and black eyeliner ran down her cheeks.

Her hair looked like the nest of a Bowerbird and her clothes looked as though someone had ripped them-off of her and then put them back her inside-out. She was barefooted and her feet were bruised and bloody as well. Billy carefully guided her over to the desk chair that he pulled up to the lavatory. He then filled the sink with hand towels and warm water then gently washed her face, taking great care not to rub her too vigorously. When he had finished cleaning her face and hands, he washed her feet. He retrieved a new set of towels from the tub and patted her dry. Grabbing the ice bucket off of the desk he turned and said to her, "I'll be right back. Don't you move!"

In a moment he was back with the ice bucket filled with ice. He poured the contents into the sink inside of a towel and ran some cold water crushing ice with the base of a coke bottle, making a crude ice-pack. He gently placed it on her right eye which now had closed shut. She winced at the coldness of the ice but held it in place while he retrieved some Band-Aids from his shaving kit and began applying them to her more serious scrapes and cuts. He handed her a hot cup of coffee that he had brewed and then wrapped her in a blanket from his bed. She took several sips of the hot coffee and he could see some color coming back to her ashen face.

"Now, you wanna talk about what happened to you tonight?" he said. "I c-can't". She trembled, her bottom lip quivered uncontrollably. "Mmm..." he muttered. "But, you must tell me what happened." She shook her head from side to side, her hair cascading over her face. She stared into her cup of coffee in her lap, lost in thought. "Well, I can tell you the cops are gonna want to know what happened." he said flatly. "NO! No Policia, puh-leeze, no poleece" She began to cry and shake all over. "OK, alright" he said. "No Federales. But you must tell me" he insisted. "It was Dom Diablo, wasn't it?" he offered. She looked up at him, her eyes wide with fear. "Ye-yes" she replied. "I figured as much. You sure you don't wanna tell me what happened?"

She placed the coffee on the lavatory and sunk back into the chair, her arms dangling at her sides. Slowly she began to tell me what had taken place. She said that Dom had discovered her love affair with a young Latino-lad who worked for him as a driver. They had met and over time had fallen in love. They had been carrying-on a secret romance for months and until tonight they had kept it a secret from everyone. However, she had confided in one of her friends. This friend had covered for her on several occasions so that she could meet her lover. But recently she had become concerned for her own safety fearing Dom might ultimately discover that she had been a willing and complicit accomplice in the subterfuge. Apparently the friend had confided in Dom and he became so enraged that he shot and killed her, making her an example of what happens to someone who seeks to work behind his back, to lie and withhold information from him.

The only reason she wasn't killed as well was because she was more valuable alive; because she was pretty, had an attractive figure, and was highly sought after by 'Johns" and other clients alike. As a result, she demanded more money than the rest of his stable of women. But now, since she had run away from him tonight she was certain that Dom would kill her when he found her, and he would ultimately find her. She said that if Billy was around when Dom came for her he would kill him also. "Let me handle, Dom-de-Dom-Dom" Billy sang. She looked at him inquisitively, as if he were crazy. And, he was crazy. But, he knew that he had an unresolved issue with Dom, and he knew that Dom wasn't the kinda guy that left unresolved issues lying around for someone else to resolve. It wasn't good business for a man in his line of work. Dom controlled his kingdom through fear and intimidation, that was his stock-in-trade and he wasn't about to let me off the hook.

Billy figured he might as well meet him on his terms. This new element just made it more moral by adding a "right-thing-to-do" measure. In any event, elements outside of his control, as so often are the case in one's life, had set the course for a head-on collision with chance, destiny or fate? It didn't matter. Call what you will, but Billy was about to have an inevitable encounter from which there was no possible retreat;

an encounter that would end with the death of one or both of them. Billy looked her in the eye and asked straight out, "I gotta know...how you got into my room? Did you have a key? She answered, "Yes, Dom has pass keys to the motel. He had given her one to keep and use when she was to sneak into a "John's" room. Billy thought he would quiz Jorge about that when this was all over.

It was now 2:30AM, and all was quiet in Little Mexico. The parking lot was empty except for the usual cars and trucks scattered about. Billy figured Dom would be coming back pretty soon and he had no time to waste in preparation. As he pondered his dilemma, the Hitchcock thriller, "Rear Window" came to my mind. he remembered James Stewart's character was a man who had suffered a broken leg and was confined to a hospital bed. He lay in the dark awaiting a killer to enter his room, armed with nothing more than a camera and a handful of flash bulbs. Where is Jimmy Stewart when you need him, he thought.

One thing was certain, he was gonna need a lot more than a camera and a handful of flash bulbs if he was gonna survive a late-night encounter with Dom Diablo…."Dom-de-Dom-Dom!" he hummed, chuckling to himself. Gotta say one thing about ol' Gringo, he's got himself a sense of humor, weird but still..? he just hoped he would have it when this night was over.

Billy anticipated that Dom would not come alone. That meant at least two attackers if not more. There was only one way in, and that being through the door. That meant there was only one way out, unless you count the large window in front. No place to hide. No place to run. Had to stay and fight, but how?! Billy recalled a famous quote of Teddy Roosevelt, his favorite president. It was a maxim he lived by, "Do what you can, with what you have, where you are" That certainly applied to Billy's situation.

Billy figured that Dom would not be the first guy through the door. He'd have one of his guys in front. he needed to find a way to disable the first wave. Since they have pass keys there won't be a need to kick in the door. "*Hmm...*" he muttered as he considered his predicament. Instantly a plan came to mind. Billy had often pondered this strategy since childhood and, for reasons that will soon become apparent; had never put it to the test, but there was no better time than the present, he imagined. He filled the ice bucket with water and poured the contents onto the pavement in front of his room. Looking at the small puddle, he deduced it would be insufficient for his needs. This plan, if it were to work, would require saturation. He soaked some bath towels and placed them in front of the door, hoping it wouldn't draw suspicion. He then cut the cord to his bed-stand lamp near where it entered the base of the lamp and made sure it would reach from the door to the wall socket. It didn't. "Shit!" He grumbled, Murphy (Law) was on the job as was to be expected. He then cut the other lamp cord at both ends. Splicing the two cords together, He then measured again, and it reached. Good. "Fuck you, Murphy!" Next he attached the raw end of the two spliced cords to the doorknob of the room door and measured once more just to be certain it would plug into the wall socket near the desk. Satisfying himself that the first line of defense was plausible, he was still concerned about the volume of water and making it appear as a natural occurrence rather than a contrivance which might alert his assailants to a possible trap. Just then another idea popped into his cranium. He went to the ice machine located in the breezeway and, with a great deal of effort, was able to move the behemoth just far enough away from the wall for him to puncture the water line leading to it with his trusty ice pick, an invaluable tool to have with you when on the road traveling. Two more holes in the copper line produced a steady stream which quickly began to cover the concrete breezeway with water. This flow soon reached the sidewalks running along either side of the motel. Excellent! Billy shoved the big ice machine back against the wall. Having accomplished his first phase of the plan, he headed back to his room where the water was already nearing the door.

Back in his room he dragged the writing table into the bathroom; it was a tight fit, but it was just what he needed. Then, instructing the girl to enter the bathroom he told her to close and lock the door behind her. Once inside, she would place the table between the door and the tub, wedging it so as to render access to her impossible thus she would be safe from intrusion. She was then told to lie down in the tub and stay in that position until such time as it was safe to come-out, that being when she heard the sound of his voice signaling an all clear. He then took the straight-backed desk chair and proceeded to break it sufficiently to remove the legs. With his knife he whittled on one end in the form of a crude hand-grip. Now he would have a short club to yield in one hand while in his other hand would be his trusty ice pick. Club and stab was his offensive strategy. He laid the remains of the chair on top of the bed.

Next on his To-Do-List was to cut strips of carpet from the floor. The same carpet he vowed to never walk on bare-footed was now being cut into strips and covering his arms. No time to be queasy with thoughts of 30-year old toe-jam. More important things to think about like life and limb. He attached the carpeting to his arms and around his neck using the sash cords from the big window to secure it. He didn't much like the thought of that nasty-ass carpet being strapped to his body, but he didn't much like the thought of being dead either. Billy hope that the carpet would protect him from broken glass or any other sharp edged instruments

When he had completed this task he stripped the ends of the lamp cord wire exposing 4 or 5 inches of raw copper wiring that he then attached to the door handle of the room. Once it was secured he plugged the makeshift wire into the wall socket. Now he was all set. He positioned himself in the corner between the headboard of the bed and the large window behind the curtains which were half-opened. From this vantage point he could see the drama unfold in seclusion.

Sitting there alone in the dark awaiting the inevitable he pondered what might be the outcome of tonight's venture. Would he be the victor or would he be the defeated foe which meant he would be dead, D-O-A. He thought about his family, his wife and his children, one by one and the possibility that he might never see them again. He was frightened beyond belief, and too angry to weep. He was in the unenviable situation where a person must decide to flee or fight, but since fleeing was not an option he was gonna fight; and with all the strength he could muster. This Dom Diablo Sonavabitch, was not gonna take him away from his family without a fight; a fight to the death. Billy reasoned he had a lot more to lose than Dom did and he thought that might give him an edge.

Finally, he said prayers again, trying not to make his plea sound like a jail-house confession, but an earnest prayer of supplication for aid in a battle of good over evil. Now, he was ready spiritually, mentally and physically and, with a plan of action. He was ready to meet his fate whatever it might be. Billy was determined to succeed or die trying; either way he would leave some indelible marks on his adversaries. Just in case things didn't go as planned he was also prepared to meet his Lord. "Okay!" He confessed out loud, "I am ready for you,

Dom Diablo, you Sonavabitch, you. Bring it on!"

THE DEVIL'S AT THE DOOR

Mercifully, he didn't have a long wait. A shadow of a man appeared against the window slowly and cautiously moving forward followed by another, two men, no more. He breathed a sigh of relief, not certain, but he felt a surge in confidence at that sight. When the first man reached the door he stopped and turned to the second man. Muffled words were exchanged, followed by a loud snap. The lights in the parking lot flickered, then dimmed and went out, an ear-splitting shriek broke the dead calm of night as the startled and electrified assailant grasped the door handle and was immediately galvanized to it in agonizing pain as a sufficient charge of voltage coursed through his body making him a non-contender. The second man startled by the torment of his companion writhing in agony didn't fully comprehend the events unfolding before him quickly enough to react except in disbelief.

Billy didn't want to give him a chance to gather his thoughts either. Crashing through the glass window with the chair he had to be certain that the glass was broken and he could jump through the window safely without cutting himself or worse yet having a section of heavy plate glass dropping on him like a guillotine and seriously cutting or killing him. The slight delay hampered his surprise somewhat, but in all the confusion Billy was upon Dom before he could regain his composure. In an instant, Billy was clubbing and stabbing his way furiously at Dom. Billy's first blow with the chair leg had caught Dom on the forearm and he had dropped his pistol, the second blow landed firmly across his upper back. Billy had just missed his neck by inches, a blow that would have killed him, and a blow that should have minimally rendered him unconscious. But it didn't and now Dom was doubled over and facing Billy, who hesitated long enough to give Dom the chance to lung at Billy like a cornered animal pinning him against the wall of the motel. Both men struggled to retrieve the fallen pistol. Unable to reach it himself, Billy flung at it with his foot and felt his shoe make contact with the heavy barrel, sending the weapon skittering several feet away from them.

Dom was able to break away from Billy's grasp, stepping backward and away from him awkwardly. Then, measuring Billy momentarily he countered with another lunging blow to Billy's mid-section. This was followed in quick succession by several jabs; in an attempt to groin punch Billy. Mercifully the punches were high, but they felt like being hit with a hammer. Then there were two quick jabs to his upper body which Billy managed to partially deflect. Another lunge from Dom smashed the back of Billy's head against the concrete wall, a blow that produced blinding light and dazed him temporarily. Dom now held Billy's head between his hands and was attempting to gouge out his eyes with his thumbs. Instinctively, Billy brought up a knee and sharply delivered the punch that Dom had failed to make in Billy's groin. Dom staggered, backing away from Billy in agony, cursing profoundly. Billy leaned against the wall in an effort to shake-off the effects from Dom's assault to his head and eyes. Dom was attempting to right himself when Billy charged at him, swinging wildly with just the pic now striking him only superficially but enough times to give Billy a slight advantage. Dom was now on the defensive and unable to attack him further.

Turning his attention to the pistol Dom made a desperate attempt and dove toward it. Billy followed instantly; raining blow after blow upon him, but Dom had managed to retrieve the weapon. A loud explosion rang out and Billy felt the sting as shards of concrete sprayed his face as the slug tore into the pavement inches from him before ricocheting harmlessly away. In quick succession two more shots, the first of which went off into the night sky, followed by a third. Instantly, Billy felt a searing pain in his left side which halted his attack. He reeled against the sudden shock of the bullet and thought he might black out. Clutching his side, he staggered backward a couple of steps.

Dom was now bent over in a crouched position again, in obvious pain, clotted blood streamed from his face in long strands dotting the pavement at his feet.

Holding the pistol in his hand, he wiped the blood from his mouth with the sleeve of his jacket. Now, looking straight into Billy's eyes he said, "Say your prayers, you fucking gringo." Billy could only watch in fear as Dom leveled the pistol at him and pulled the trigger. Billy heard the hammer fall, then "Click!" At that moment God answered his prayers and intervened on his behalf. The gun had jammed or misfired, it didn't matter which. Fighting the pain in his side he leapt upon his adversary with renewed vigor and savagery.

In a fury Billy pummeled him with a terrible unrelenting assault. It proved to be too much for Dom to withstand. He collapsed to his knees dropping the pistol for the second and last time. Once again, Dom attempted to stand, but his knees wouldn't support him. He stumbled forward a step. Then twisting violently on his heels he fell backward onto the pavement. He lay there moaning in agony. Billy took no chances and was astride his chest looking down upon the battered and bloody face of his foe. Dom gazed back at Billy with fire in his eyes, spitting blood as he cursed him in Spanish, "Vete al infierno, Gringo! Pudrete en el infierno. No Dom. Not tonight. Not ever!" Billy countered. And with those fatal words Billy plunged the icepick into his chest up to its hilt, just below the sternum. He felt the tip glance off bone and then go deep into Dom's flesh where his heart should be. Dom's head lurched violently then, as a whale would upon surfacing from the depths expel air from his blowhole, Dom gasped a final puff of blood as air escaped his lungs and he breathed his last.

Billy looked over to see if the other assailant was gonna be a threat, but there was no chance of that; he looked like death on a cracker. Billy rolled off of Dom and lay on the wet pavement next to him gazing up into the starless night. He felt the stinging, burning pain in his side return. He was light headed and nauseous, beaten and bloody, but he was alive. He could hear voices, lots of voices, people speaking Spanish, people running to and fro. He seemed to be in a vortex, pandemonium was all about him. Then, out of the night came lights and sirens followed by people in uniforms.

Soon he found himself inside an ambulance being tended to by a young Paramedic. Billy looked up over the oxygen mask covering his face and asked, "Am I gonna die?" The paramedic laughed and replied, "Not tonight my man. You took a bullet in the side but it didn't hit any major organs or anything near as we can tell, just relax. We'll be at the hospital in a minute. You're gonna be fine" Billy lay on the gurney listening to the siren.

He closed his eyes. Visions of his wife and children drifted into his mind. He could see their happy faces calling out to him. Then, he lost consciousness.

THE AFTERMATH

The next day when Billy awoke in the hospital a nurse was standing over him smiling. "Well, good morning, big guy. It looks like our hero has awakened", she announced to the room. Billy caught a glimpse of his wife, behind the nurse beaming a smile as tears ran down her cheeks. Then a police detective neared the bed and introduced himself. He wanted to discuss what had happened last night, what had led up to the altercation. Billy's wife took his hand in hers and stroked his brow. They didn't speak, but only gazed into each other's eyes and it was then that Billy realized his ordeal was really over. When he had finished recounting the story for the detective he said that Billy's version corroborated the statements given by the witnesses. He had interviewed Jorge and the Mexican girl, Carmelita Estevez, last night at the scene. He assured Billy that there would be no charges filed against him. It was a clear case of self-defense.

His last night in the hospital was serene. After he had finished an early supper and the orderly had retrieved his tray he asked his wife to fix him a glass of lemonade. She poured some ice in a glass and filled it with water. Then, taking a Crystal Light pouch from her purse she tore open the top and poured the contents into the glass. A brisk stir of the water and the crystals quickly dissolved. She handed him the glass and Billy took a sip. Ah, cool, tart, refreshing. Billy then gulped down the remaining drink and handed her the glass, smacking my lips. "Never tasted better." She smiled and said, "Anything else? Yeah, will you turn off all the lights in the room; I wanna get some much needed shut-eye. You got it, kid. I'm gonna sit over there in that monstrosity of a chair and check my email. I'm certain I've got a ton of mail to answer." Billy didn't respond. He pulled the covers up to his neck. The dark room was cool and quiet save for the hissing sound of oxygen.

Billy looked at his wife sitting in the large overstuffed chair. The only light was that of her iPhone which bathed the contours of her worried face in an eerie glow; her soft features appeared disembodied like, the face in the magic mirror in "Snow White and the Seven Dwarfs." He studied her eyes as she scanned the data she was retrieving from her email server. They were full of purpose, darting back and forth over the lines of text as if she were searching for a special message or code. Billy smiled contentedly and closed his eyes.

JUSTIFICATION

Suddenly and quite unexpectedly Billy's thoughts raced back to the night in the parking lot of the Americana Inn grappling in the dark with Dom. Billy's body stiffened as he relived those final terrible moments. He had not thought of that night since the morning after when he awoke to the face of a charming nurse and a pleasant but very serious Hangman detective.

Now in the quiet darkness of his room and immersed in his thoughts he came face to face with the unalterable facts of that night. He had deliberately and purposely taken a man's life. He had watched him die and witnessed the light go out in his eyes as he gasped that final breath there on the wet pavement on that moonless night. Was he justified in doing what he did? He remembered the words of William Munny. "It's a hell of a thing, killing a man. (You)

Take away all he's got and all he's ever gonna have." He let them sink into his cortex with new meaning.

But then Billy reasoned, if he had not killed Dom that night Dom would have surely killed him, if not that night, then certainly later. And if it had been later and his family was present he most surely would have killed them all as well. Yet, still there was that brief moment where Billy, sitting astride Dom's body entered into that final terse exchange of words, and did willfully act as judge, jury and executioner, by plunging his icepick into Dom's heart. Billy felt both guilt and anger arising out of the dilemma his thoughts had created. What followed was a period of vexing consternation in which he argued vehemently with his inner man Billy achieved a moment of clarity where he was one hundred percent certain that he had acted out of flight or fight. And, since flight had not been an option he had been thrust into the arena in a do or die confrontation.

However, the combatants that night battled for two very different reasons. Billy fought to preserve his life, while Dom fought to take it from him. In that context with everything else being equal a decided edge would have go to the participant who was fighting for his life. Therefore, Billy argued, he did what had to be done. Dom had brought that night and the inevitable and final consequences of its events upon himself. Billy's actions in light of those facts were justified and he was, therefore, blameless in the eyes of God and man.

As a result of his reaching that decision he vowed to put that night behind him. There would never be a time from this point on that he would have to relive its horror. He opened his eyes and stared at the ceiling, allowing his emotions to reconcile with his reasoning. He felt a calming peace come over him, an affirmation of his reasoning. He took another, reassuring glance at his wife, still engrossed in her emails, and closed his eyes.

HOMEWARD BOUND

The next morning Billy was discharged from the hospital. Arriving at the front entrance he was confronted by a TV news crew and a pretty blonde reporter. He answered a few questions before his wife finally interceded for him and got him into the car. The news lady thrust a microphone at Billy before he had a chance to close the door and asked, "Mr. Hightower, if you had to do it again, would you? Do it again, that is." Billy's reply was short, "Damn right I would; except this time I'd dodge that last shot." She smiled a big toothy grin as the door gently closed.

His wife eased the car away from the curb and the gathering throng of people. Exiting the hospital parking lot she turned onto Navarre Street, and then she took a left onto Houston Highway that led out of town to Highway 59 and Houston. Barring any more catastrophes they would at a cousin's house where Billy could convalesce. Drive time would take about 4-hours, less knowing his wife's penchant for the lead foot. Billy set the seat back into a reclined position and closed his eyes.

"You OK, baby?" his wife asked. He nodded and managed a smile. "Yeah, I'm good." She smiled back and affectionately brushed the back of her hand across his battered cheek. Billy grimaced slightly as she did. "Oh! I'm sorry, honey. Does it hurt bad? Naw, only when I laugh. Haw!" she guffawed. "So, you're pretty much pain free then, right? Oh! Funny, very funny" he replied, "I'm working on it, though." he continued, "What? She replied, "The pain or the laughter? Oh how I've missed your snappy repartee." They both laughed and he grimaced again. "See!" He said. "OK" enough of that she smiled, "Do you want anything? Are you hungry or thirsty?"

Nope, I'm just fine" he answered. "Well, you just settle back and relax. Try to get some sleep. OK? OK!" he smiled back at her and closed his eyes once again.

The pain in his side wasn't a distraction. The pleasing fragrance of his wife filled the car reinforcing his sense of security and reminding him of her constant presence. He lay motionless, listening to the rhythm of the road, the drumming sound of the highway, the thumping of expansion joints, pleasantly familiar sounds, reassuring and strangely comforting. It wasn't long before Billy drifted off to sleep.

fini

A NIGHT IN THE WOODS
A FIRE IN THE SKY
A MOMENT TO LIVE, A MOMENT TO DIE!

BY

A. S. WEST

THE BEGINNING~

I grew up in South Louisiana, Cajun country, in a little rural town practically dead-center in the south half of the state, just west of the great Atchafalaya Basin. LaSalle was a wonderful place in which to live and to grow up. In the early 1950's there were about 25,000 people living in and around LaSalle. Thinking back it was a simpler time and a time when people seemed to enjoy life more. It certainly wasn't as hectic as life is today. Divorce was a rare occurrence. Mothers stayed at home for child rearing and to provide a pleasant environment for their family. Violent crime wasn't an issue so house doors were seldom locked.

On weekends, holidays, and summer vacations, we had much greater latitude with respect to our personal time and activities. In a time without smart phones it wasn't necessary that we check-in every hour. We would tell out parents where we were going and what we might be doing, and they would tell us when we were expected to be home...usually an hour before supper. In many ways it was as though we lived on a different planet altogether in comparison to today's lifestyle. Most working people went home for lunch which usually was the largest meal of the day. Supper consisted of leftover lunch items. For a typical   lunch,

Cajun women would prepare fried, stewed, roasted or baked meat (hamburger, chicken, pork, or fish). Items that were included on every table at every meal were: a pot of rice and gravy. Vegetables were plentiful; Beans, Peas, Corn, Okra; real ice-tea; a plate of sliced tomatoes with mayonnaise on the side; a loaf of "Evangeline Maid" bread, with a slab of butter; and desserts, included cakes, cookies, brownies or other sweets, all home-made. Other staples were: chicken & sausage gumbo or seafood gumbo, Etoufee of shrimp or crawfish (in season), smoked sausage, Andouille, Boudin, Jambalaya, Red beans & rice, Stuffed Bell peppers or Cabbage Rolls, and many others dishes.

A typical work week looked like this: Monday, Tuesday, and Wednesday morning until noon; Thursday, Friday, and Saturday morning until noon. And, in the smaller towns that dotted the countryside... around LaSalle on Sundays there were far more horse-drawn carriages tied up in front of the local church than there were automobiles. French was spoken in practically every household, particularly among the elderly, and grandparents. People acted happier and visited others frequently. Greetings included sayings such as these: "Mais, how y'all are?: Y'all get down and come inside; How's yo' mama and dem'? Comment ça va?

Those days, the LaSalle area economy was primarily farming. Big oil had come to town, but it hadn't captured the economy as it did in the ensuing years. Field crops were Sugar Cane, Rice, Cotton, Sweet Potatoes (Yams), Corn, and a mix of Beans (not soy) and Peas. There were a lot of small farms and ranches. For those of you city-slickers who may not know the difference between them, farms grow field-crops; ranches grow livestock, cattle, horses, poultry but mostly beef cattle. Beef cattle in the area were a mix of breeds, Angus, Herefords, Limousins, and Brahma, but most were Cracker cattle or Swamp Cattle as they're called in Louisiana.

Swamp cattle are a breed of cattle that were introduced in the 16th Century by the Spaniards, first in Florida and then along the Gulf coast. These small cattle, by comparison, are a most hardy and durable breed that has flourished in the 500-years since they were introduced to the New World. The following incident occurred in the same time period and is representative of events of the day. Insofar as Swamp cattle are concerned as it is an example of their ability to endure the hostile environs found along our Gulf coast.

Louisiana has always been pestered by mosquitoes. In the years leading up to the 20th century, mosquitoes were responsible for the spread and devastation of Yellow-Fever in which many, many thousands died.

However, after the last epidemic ended in 1905, and scientists at last discovered the role that mosquitoes played in the spread of that disease, yellow-fever ceased to be a problem. While the plague may be history its carrier remains to plague Louisianans' to this day The mosquitoes that rise up out of the marshes of our fair state must have been mutated by some devilish fiend operating deep in our swamps for these critters are large...much larger than your average 'skeeter. These bad girls (everyone knows it's just the females that bite you, right?) Well these ladies don't bite...they sting when they stick you! And, if you should squish one, they'll virtually explode with blood. Ugh, disgusting!

On this particular day I am seated in a duck blind in the marshes of Vermilion Parish, Louisiana, approaching that time referred to by duck hunters as the "Magic Moment", that moment when the first glint of light appears on the horizon signaling the opening of the day's hunting. It is at that time of day when your eyes begin scanning the horizon for flights of ducks. I don't see any ducks, but what I do see is a small, impenetrable cloud drifting my way. I recognize it as a swarm of marsh 'skeeters. Now, I'm talking about 'skeeters that make you shrink in fear when you first observe their size and their ferocity. The only thing between me and the oncoming cloud of blood-thirsty insects is a thin veil of netting covering my face.

No part of my flesh is exposed to this threat. Behind my veil I watch intently. This wasn't my first time to suffer such an assault. Nevertheless, no matter how many times one experiences these encounters it is not lacking in drama. The swarm, numbering in the thousands has now enveloped me, completely covering the netting over my face as the 'skeeters frantically attempt to reach my flesh. A barely perceptible sound occurs accompanied by a slight, discernible movement in the netting each time 'skeeters strike it. A person suffering from claustrophobia would no doubt panic under this onslaught.

Fortunately as the sun breaks free from the horizon the swarm dissipates and moves off in search of another less protected victim. No wonder these critters have been known to drive elephants crazy in Africa. But this ain't Africa, Leroy, although it just as soon as be. From this memory I'm teleported to an earlier time-line, a summer day when I accompanied my dad to Cameron, Louisiana, the parish seat for, Cameron Parish.

It was late summer of '57 and the memories and effects of Hurricane Audrey were fresh on everyone's mind and the horrific evidence of that cataclysmic event was everywhere still. I don't know what ground-zero looks like and I hope I never do, but I imagine it looks an awful lot like what I saw that day. Cameron (orig. Leesburg) is, was and always will be nothing more than a fishing village and jumping-off spot for offshore oil. It's hard to believe that anyone would really want to live in Cameron, in fact statistics show otherwise. However, the town stands as a testament to man's will having barely survived at least fourteen (14) hurricanes, three (3) catastrophic hurricanes beginning with the unforgettable Hurricane Audrey in 1957, which claimed over 500 lives, followed by Hurricane Rita in 2005, and

Hurricane Ike in 2008. Little wonder the town's population is down 80% since 2000.

The town itself is situated near the heel of the Louisiana coastline just south of Calcasieu Lake. The landscape was littered with wreckage. Mobile homes, which were in abundance, were all destroyed as was every other commercial or residential structure. Trees sheared in half or uprooted lay everywhere along with broken telephone poles. Twisted metal from buildings and signage were scattered far and wide including pieces or parts of machinery, cars, and boats, small and large dotted the landscape. The most dominant structure in the town, for that matter the only structure was the weather-beaten courthouse which was to Cameron what the Super Bowl was to New Orleans in providing a place of refuge for displaced citizenry during ruinous hurricane disasters.

The reason the carnage was so severe in the case of Audrey, was that those days were before the weather alerts we now have. The residents of Cameron were caught completely unaware of the impending doom that was to befall them. As a hurricane, Audrey was not all that severe, but its tidal surge, a wall of water 12-feet high was devastating. The residents were still recovering from its effects. Fishing boats and tug-boats of enormous size were found twenty miles from the coast. Practically every structure in Audrey's path was washed away, save the courthouse building.

My dad was buying Oil & Gas leases for Texaco at that time and he had scheduled meetings with some mineral owners that afternoon. People were desperate for money so my dad was welcomed with open arms by the Cajun owners. Before his meetings we went to the courthouse and I had the privilege of "pulling books" for him. Here's a back breaking exercise if ever there was one. Now for those of you who don't know, back in those days the record books and their indices (plural for index, although now they're simply referred to as indexes) of the Clerk of Court's Records were books made for the Nephilim (look it up, but basically, "Giants"). I don't know whose idea it was to create 40-pound books the size of the hood on a Buick "Roadmaster"? There had to be reasoning behind that idea, but what? I still can't figure that one out?

In those days the clerks had to transcribe each recorded document into these books, while the original documents were stored in a vault. Thankfully, with the advent of copiers and later computers these books were downsized to a much more manageable size and for all intents and purposes eliminating the "heavy lifting" of those days. The indexes were laid out on slant-topped (?) counters and were organized by year and last name…Vendor/Vendee. My dad ran the indexes and would then hand me a piece of paper with the books containing the instrument he needed to peruse. I swear he managed to find a way so that each book I had to retrieve was either on the very bottom shelf or the very top shelf. After hoisting, delivering and replacing some twenty or so books I was ready to take a break.

We finally did break for lunch and ended up at I believe the only restaurant in town at that time. After lunch we ventured out into the hinterlands along Highway 27 (Creole Nature Trail) towards Creole, Louisiana, a place where "wide spot in the road" is being generous. After meeting with his mineral owners and getting some leases signed we began our return trip to LaSalle. It was late afternoon by then and the sun hung low in the summer sky. On the north side of the highway where many Swamp cattle grazed there were huge "smokes" built by the ranchers to protect their cattle against the daily swarms of mosquitoes. These smokes (fires intended to produce an abundance of thick, heavy smoke) were built using old trees, tires, crop residues, Neem leaves (another lookup) and other such material, and coal oil was the accelerant of choice. Cattle would stand in long lines that led up to the smokes. Several cows could be seen standing in this smoke. One group would stand in it for a couple of minutes before moving off, allowing for the next group of cows to enter the smoke. It was an amazing site to see as these creatures seemed to understand that the smoke would protect them from the mosquitoes and each instinctively knew it only had a limited time to stand in the smoke before relinquishing their place for the next cow waiting patiently in line. This was my first encounter with this practice that has been used for centuries around the world. It's not really understood what the smoke does to lessen the assault of mosquitoes, but it does seem to have a repelling effect. I think the smoke tends to mask the scent of warm bloodied mammals which makes it harder for mosquitoes to "see" us. I could be wrong?

About halfway between Creole and nowhere, which is about 10-miles in any direction from BFE, the car swerved suddenly followed by that sickening sound of thump-thump-thump-thump, the sound of a tire going flat. Dad didn't bother to pull off on the shoulder because there wasn't any shoulder. Even if he had we would have really been in a fix in that soft "gumbo" loamy soil. My dad was not one to use profanity reserving such outbursts for special occasions...this was one of those occasions. There we sat staring out the windshield ahead where swarms of mosquitoes were billowing up out of the marshes.

He looked at me and said, "We'll take turns on changing this tire. I'll go first then you'll have to spell me. OK? You understand?" I nodded grimly knowing all too well that we were fixing to get out asses chewed-up by several-billion 'skeeters. I wished we could have stood in the smoke at that moment. Dad got out, managed to open the trunk and unscrew the foot of the jack which secured the spare in place, and was able to set the jack before succumbing to the onslaught of the mosquitoes. He looked like he was a madman dancing the jitterbug as he swatted the cloud of unrelenting bugs covering him. Finally, he was back in the car bringing a small swarm with him. "Alright, son, you're up." I took a deep breath and jumped into the fray.

I had no idea what I was getting into. The mosquitoes were everywhere...in my eyes, in my nose, my ears, my mouth...it was, to say the least, horrific. I managed only to get the car partially jacked up before I had to surrender. Dad was back out and he managed to remove the flat tire, I was back out securing the tire with the lug-wrench which was a slow, tiresome exercise, but by now I had become a madman as well cursing and swatting the air wildly as I struggled to tighten the last lug nut in place. Dad finished up for us, throwing the flat tire into the trunk along with the tools.

By the time we arrived back home we had scratched ourselves raw. That night I slept without bed covers as my entire body was alive with itchiness. Much later, I finally drifted off to sleep, the smell of calamine lotion hanging heavy in the air.

Now back to the types of cattle found in Louisiana in those days, ca.1950 ...and there were Dairy cows which were primarily Holstein. At least that's what I remember mostly was Holsteins, I know there were others. On the horse side, it was Quarter Horses for riding, roping, and racing... and very few if any Thoroughbreds. In between those categories, there was a little bit of everything else, from vegetable farming to hog farming. The countryside around LaSalle obviously reflected the farming industry, mostly pastures and fields, but there were also vast wooded areas as well particularly along Coulees (small creek or stream, from the French word, "to flow") and along the bayous and rivers as well as other places.

In the old days land was always attached or bounded on one side or other but water, the staff of life, for crops and cattle but equally important for travel, for there were no roads in those days. Everything moved on water. And the timber that grew in large stands along the banks of these waterways and in the water was vitally important for construction of houses, barns, fence posts, furniture and the like, and for burning in fireplaces or stoves. Bald Cypress, Tupelo Gum, Oaks are predominate in the swamps or wetlands. Further inland, Live Oaks, Southern Pine, Water Oaks, Pecan, Hackberry, Gum, and on and on. The list is extensive.

The early land grant tracts on the Mississippi River ran from the river back towards the wetlands or swamp. These were also found along the navigable streams of southern Louisiana, and as we as along major waterways in other areas. These were known as French arpent land divisions (Arpent: a measure of land equal to 0.85 acres of land). These are long narrow parcels of land four-sided, but pie-shaped, ranging from 2 to 8 arpents on the frontage (river side) and usually 40-arpents deep. This method of land division provided each land-owner with river frontage as well as land suitable for cultivation and habitation. Typically, the rear boundary was covered with bottomland woods or swamp, but needless to say, with a heavy growth of timber.

In the 1950's, people hunted lands freely, although it was cordial to stop in to see the landowner and to make certain he was okay with your being on his property. Usually speaking if the land wasn't posted it was OK to hunt on it. Often times the land owner was harvesting his own crop for his and his family's needs. This could mean Alligators or maybe doves or ducks, but in any event those certain species that were forbidden and you couldn't take any of them without incurring the landowner's wrath. If you hunted an owner's property, you took care to be respectful in your conduct, noting where livestock was located and closing and latching any gates you may have opened. Species such as squirrels or rabbits were okay to hunt almost anywhere. If you had a good days hunt you might leave a couple of ducks, or some doves or squirrels for the owner.

It is illegal to take any Robins, but in our younger years we shot many a Robin and

Blackbirds as well. Robins are excellent eating birds and we had many a meal off our takes...we'd breast'em out like doves and cook them over an open fire. Good eating! So, it was in this environment that we tramped through and over untold hundreds of miles of farmland and woods, seeking adventure wherever we went.

There was a camp belonging to the Popler family that was located southwest of LaSalle on Saloon Road that was a favorite place from which we conducted a great many of our forays into the countryside. Brent Popler and his older brother Cary were both good friends of mine and I was a regular visitor to their camp for many years. Across Saloon Road were lands belonging to the Burgan family that extended from the opposite side of Saloon Road facing Popler's Camp to the Little Red River, a distance of about a quarter mile, more or less. A gravel road permitted access from Saloon Road to the river where the Burgans had a large camp. The road was covered by a thick canopy of trees and ground cover on either side so dense as to obscure the road altogether. We explored this property regularly often-times stopping at an isolated, old pond about 50 to 60-paces west of the gravel road. This pond was so secluded that it would go unnoticed walking past it if one weren't aware of its presence. It was about a three acre pond, no more than waist deep and home to a large frog population.

We frequently made stops there to look for the possibility of any snakes slinking about. Wherever you find an abundance of frogs, you'll also find snakes and Snake hunting, for a time, was one of the main reasons for our venturing into the woods. We hunted snakes with a passion, the Popler brothers, and Mike Montague and me. Occasionally Rex Verot joined us. All of us at one time or another had king snakes as pets, usually the speckled or salt and pepper variety. But we didn't limit our snake exploits to capturing non-venomous snakes; we also hunted and killed many water-moccasins or cottonmouths (so named for their white mouths) and also copperheads which were not as plentiful as cottonmouths.

After dispatching the snake's head we'd skin'em out and keeping their hides as trophies to display or for use on belts or hat bands. We'd stretch the skins out on wooden planks attaching them with upholstery tacks. Once stretched we'd scrape the skin gently removing any excess meat or fat. A thin layer of salt was then evenly applied before placing the skins in the sun for curing which usually took about a week. Once the skin had dried thoroughly we'd remove all of the salt with warm water. Next, we'd gently rub a mixture of alcohol and glycerin to both sides of the skins to insure they would be supple. Then, we'd hang them in a closet on a piece of clothesline using clothespins until completely cured. The skin would then be rolled and placed in a cool, dry place for storage for a couple of weeks.

And, that's how we did it back in the '50's. At the height of my snake killing days I had a large cardboard box full of skins, squirrel tails and crow's feet. The crow's feet were stretched so that the toes were splayed and the lower leg was upright. After a few days the foot would be attached to a piece of wood and the wood would then be glued to a piece of rock, making an interesting paperweight. I wish I still had that box today.

In any event, once we were on a snake we would pursue it until we had it cornered or until it finally turned on us in a threatening maneuver. We always carried hiking poles or snake poles made from a stout tree limb whose base was sufficiently wide enough to trap a snake's body under it. Once we had the snake's neck beneath the base of our pole we would then grab it as close to its head as possible. Thinking back we were pretty daring in our handling of these poisonous snakes, but we were always very careful to make sure we had a tight grip behind the head clamping the neck between our index finger and thumb and holding the body extended in our free hand to keep it from coiling around the "hot" hand, the one holding the snake's head. If we were going to release the snake, which was unusual, nonetheless caution had to be taken as a release could be as hazardous as a capture.

The best method to insure that the snake wouldn't strike you during release was to separate yourself from the snake as quickly as possible which meant standing sideways and flinging the snake head first across your chest.

As an aside: All our snake handling skills were self-taught in the field. We learned just by doing them; scary huh? Do you think our parents ever inquired about our handling of these snakes? Uh-uh! My mama used to tell her friends how she'd go out and replenish the salt on the skins laying out on the top of the pump-house (in those days we lived in an area where we had well water and each well had a pump unit which was housed in a small shed, the size of a large dog-house. I laid my skins out on the top of the pump-house for drying.) But our snake hunting days came to an abrupt end one summer day when Brent was bitten on the hand by a water-moccasin and big brother, Cary, rushed him to the hospital. I visited Brent the next day in the hospital and was stunned to find that his had swollen to the size of a catcher's mitt. Who would have known a hand could swell to such proportions? Brent recovered fully, but that incident ended for good our zest for snake killing.

However, long before that fateful day, we were all spending a weekend at the Popler camp. it was the summer of '58, as I recall. Cary, Brent, Mike, Rex and I were reminiscing about our day. We had filled it doing the usual things we did when out there which meant hiking, killing snakes and, on this occasion, floating a mile or so down the Little Red River so we could jump-off the Broussard Road Bridge. We had a couple of life-jackets we tied together and we entered the river upstream near

Burgan's camp, floating en mass downstream on the current to the bridge. At one point Brent gave chase to a fat water moccasin swimming about 10-feet in front of us, Brent got close enough to take a swipe at it with his machete, but he missed. Cottonmouths swim with their whole body on top of the water so they're real easy to spot. The snake ducked under water when Brent missed him and that freaked him and the rest of us out so we quickly abandoned the chase.

In those days the river still had barge traffic and the bridges crossing it had to compensate for the tugboats that pushed strings of barges laden with shell, rock or other composite materials up and downstream. The bridges along the river were vertical-lift bridges, bridges that lifted a section of span by way of a system of cables and counterweights which were strung from 4-lift piers, one at each corner of the span. I mention this because we were jumping from the railing of the bridge itself and some places higher up than that. We made our ascent on the bridge by climbing the protection piers jutting out into the water on either side of the bridge. These bulwarks, made of huge telephone-like poles only larger, not only protected the infrastructure of the bridge itself, but funneled the barges by guiding them into the mouth of the channel (Side Note: At this time the channel was roughly 10-feet deep and 100-feet wide) .

A couple of days later my mama casually mentioned in an off-handed sort of way, "Oh, did you boys enjoy jumping off the Broussard Road Bridge the other day?" Now my mama had a nose for everything we did especially that which we shouldn't have been doing. If we had been smoking or drinking she knew the instant we crossed the threshold of the backdoor. It wasn't until years later that we understood that cigarette smoke permeated clothing. She had a spy network in place that would have been the envy of J Edgar Hoover. As to our bridge incident, she later confessed that a friend had observed our escapade. It was then I remembered that a party barge floated past us as we were frolicking atop the bridge, but since I didn't recognize anyone on board we simply waved as they passed underneath us. This only reinforced the notion that you can never be absolutely certain that your actions would not fall under the gaze of unexpected witnesses. Add to that, my being a redhead naturally made me a stand-out from the rest of the crowd and I was well known by my parent's circle of friends.

Anyway, putting that aside, after a half hour or so of jumping off the bridge into the murky depths of the Little Red River, so called because of its red tint, we climbed the protection piers of the bridge for the last time and crossed over to the south-side of the river. We made a stop at the old country store just down the road from the bridge for cold drinks and a snack, before continuing on our hike back to the Popler camp. The old country store (whose name is lost to history) was ancient in those days. Old gravity-fed gas pumps long retired stood like silent sentinels out in front. Made almost completely of old "Pecky" Cypress boards. The old store creaked and groaned with every step you'd take. Inside you could find damn near everything from donuts to dynamite. In the back of the store were two double-wide doors opening onto a loading dock where grain, feed and supplies went in and out. In the summer, the doors were kept open all day to permit a behemoth box fan which provided the best circulation of air to be found anywhere in the area. This enormous fan was capable of sucking insects, small birds, and a whole lotta air from outside. The air filtered through every crack and crevice in the store and exited right out the back, cooling the air as it went. We sat on the floor of the loading dock our legs hanging off the edge and took advantage of the coolest breeze around.

After 20-minutes or so of sitting on the loading dock our butts were pretty well stove up and we were dreading the walk back to camp. After being on the go in the heat all-day, swimming down river a couple miles and climbing and jumping off the Broussard Bridge, we were dog-ass tired; and we were still facing a hike home in the hot summer sun. From the store to the Popler camp was roughly a mile and a-half (mol). However, if we cut-off the corner at the Babineaux/Saloon Road intersect we could shorten our walk by roughly a quarter mile give or take. The only problem with this route was we had to cross the Babineaux Brahma Ranch lands. We decided it was worth it. Trudging home across the open field we could see several Brahmas in the distance gathered under the shade of a stand of life-oak trees and it looked as though they hadn't even noticed us.

Now, young men are driven by all sorts of impulses, some good, some not so good, and some just plain crazy and Mr. Crazy was about to show-up. Mike, at least I remember it being Mike, but it could well have been anyone of us. No matter, the thought occurred that it would be great fun to call-out the bulls. We had done this on several occasions and it was a great adrenaline rush to out run a Brahma bull. Of course we usually did it when we were in relatively close proximity to a fence line and in no real danger of being trampled. But this time we were 100 yards from a fence when Mike cut loose with his finest bull call. I must admit we were all very good at imitating a bull, perhaps a little too good. At first there was no discernable movement in the herd and they were still a long way off. However, with Mike's prompting our joining in with his calling, one Mr. Pissed-off bull appeared in the distance and looked to be closing the gap between him and us. Realizing 2,000-pounds of beef on the hoof was bearing down on us we mustered our strength to reach the fence line before the bull reached us. It was an amazing feat...proving once again that the human body can achieve unattainable goals with the proper inducement and incentive.

After several minutes of gasping for breath we were refreshed to the point where we could laugh about it...even brag about it. The truth of the matter be known? The bull wasn't even that close, but that didn't sit well for a good storytelling. We were always told that a Black Angus bull will go through a fence while a Brahma bull will jump it. I've seen many a Brahma bull climb the gates in rodeos so we were glad he was on his side of the fence and we were on ours.

Back at the Poplar camp at last we lounged, relaxing our wearied bodies while discussing the day's adventures and, after eating an evening meal, we decided to go out to the Bergan pond across the road and scare up a mess of bullfrogs. It was still early in the evening when we struck off. A faint whiff of honeysuckle wafted in the evening air on a light, Summer-night's breeze as Mother Earth cast off her mantle of heat from another hot, humid day. It was a relatively cool, moonless night and the natural canopy of tree limbs and foliage hanging over Burgan Road that sheltered us from the sun during the day, created the odd feeling of a descent into a cavernous tunnel. The beams from our flashlights only heightened that effect. The woods on either side of the road were alive with sound, the incessant whirring and humming of insect life, the searing rasp of night calls from the male cicadas, accompanied by the crunching of gravel under our boots. Creepy shadows created by the beams from our lights danced about us, reinforcing the eerie effect of a foreboding tunnel. We spoke little during our trek to the pond.

As we reached the take-off point to go to the pond, I was seriously considering calling it a day and going back to the camp, but I knew I'd never hear the end of that. By comparison the walk to the pond was a short trek, thank goodness, 'cause it crossed some of the thickest woods you'd ever want to walk in. Difficult as it was to cross during the day, crossing at night was a test of endurance. We hadn't gone but a few steps before we were embraced by the thick bramble of choking woods. Climbing vines reached out to entangle us in their snares, stickers and prickly vegetation snagged us, tagged us, and jabbed us. Low hanging limbs of sapling trees slapped at us and the brush of spider webs clung to our skin, amplifying the intensity of the woods as it slowly closed in around us. I felt a pressing urge to run, but I resisted for the fear of falling was very real and meant being engulfed in the unseen writhing clutches of this wooded labyrinth. In spite of that, my steps were quickened, motivated primarily by the thought of the spiders that were lurking and crawling around in the dark. These weren't your typical little wood spiders, these were Golden Orb-Weavers aka, Banana Spiders, a formidable looking spider whose very presence strikes fear in people such as me.

These arachnids are found in great abundance in the woods of South Louisiana. Now, snakes, even the poisonous ones, I could handle, literally, but spiders? Whoa Nellie! That was another thing all together. I have always been deathly afraid of spiders since my early childhood, and spiders the size of a small animal? Fugetaboutit! I found myself thinking over and over. "Banana Spiders don't really grow that big...do they?... Bull-Shit! Yes they DO!" I couldn't get my mind past the fact that as I trudged through this jungle that big spiders weren't beginning to crawl all over me. I have this recurring nightmare...which goes something like this. I'm walking down a gravel road with dense, dark woods on either side, much like the road we just walked. Music from The Twilight Zone can be heard in the background and Rod Serling is clearing his throat. A couple hours have now passed and you're walking back up that very same road. It is almost dark. Actually its dusk...meaning there's no more of that 30-minutes of light left in the day... outside, maybe, in one of the many surrounding fields, but inside on the gravel road with its natural cover and barrier of limbs and foliage, it's already dark-thirty.

Switching on a trusty flashlight a fleeting thought enters your mind, "Did you remember to replace the old batteries in your flashlight the other day, Zippy?" Up ahead the beam of your light shines on several colored objects. Drawing nearer you realize that the colored objects are in fact very large and very real spiders suspended in mid-air, about 3 to 5-feet off the ground. Panic sets in and you desperately scan the darkness with your flashlight seeking an alternate route that will steer you way clear of Spiderville. You frantically probe the tomb-like darkness with your shaky and diminishing beam of light as you discover to your horror that the roadway is a teeming mass of enormous spiders all hungry and all waiting to sink their fangs deep into the flesh of an intruder unlucky enough to trip its web. Where did all these spiders come from, anyway? How the Hell did they build these webs so quickly, anyhow...and who's the hell's in charge of this dream!? It's at that moment you realize you are totally alone, and as you recoil in abject terror you grasp a glimpse of the horrible death that awaits you.

For those of you unfamiliar with Banana Spiders let me enlighten you. They can and do build large webs in record time and they are found in great abundance as described above and they are as scary looking as the Alien Queen and her brood of spider-like face-huggers. But enough spider talk. Suffice it to say, I survived the spider gauntlet that night and after several very unnerving moments we at last break out of the bramble of woods and into the clearing where the pond is situated.

I ask Rex to use his flashlight to check for any spiders that may be on me. Rex says, "Oh! Holy shit! Do not move, man. Trust me...do not move!" The blood drains from my brain and I feel faint. "Get it off! Get it off! I scream. Rex breaks out in uncontrollable laughter. Thankfully there were none and my heart now slows from 300-bpm to a normal rate. Above us a star studded sky embraces us, covering us with a dazzling cathedral of heavenly light and reassuring us that God is in Heaven and that He had seen fit to deliver us from the snares of the dreaded woods. Gazing into the eternal depths of the universe, we stood motionless for a moment in awe of the splendor above us. Slowly our senses adjust to our terrestrial surroundings as the chorus of flora Amphibia, a cornucopia of sound swelling in a crescendo of night noise as the songs of a million peepers and tree frogs flood the air, punctuated by the intermittent croaking of bullfrogs lying in the shallows near the water's edge.

Standing upon the worn ring levee that skirts the pond the air is heavy and wet and a fine mist hovers just above the water's black surface. I was the first to step into the pond's murkiness. As it turns out I was the only one. Why am I always the first to do this kinda stuff?. What? Nobody else can do this shit? My rubber boots sink deep into the soft ooze that covered the bottom. I shined my light over its misty surface searching for large yellow eyes that should have been staring back at me along the banks and in the shallows, but there was only the impenetrable mist. Disgusted by the results I turn around to see that the rest of the team is still standing on the ring levee behind me.

At the end of the line is Cary Poplar, oblivious to everything...well, certainly oblivious to me, that's for sure.. He's too busy scanning the pond and all that part of the Parish. He's brought along his trusty 50-Billion-candle power lamp with which he is now sweeping the black night. It looked more like something you'd find mounted on a tower at "Stalag 17". If Sputnik happened to be over-head at that moment, you could rest assure the Kremlin was being notified of a strange light emanating from BFE, Louisiana. Surely Cary sees me? He must see me; I'm standing practically in front of him! Holy Mother of Blessed Searchlights! He doesn't see me! And, at that precise moment the shaft of intense, white light from his lamp burns into my retinas instantly blinding me as if a thousand make that a million, flashbulbs have gone off before me. My pupils have been reduced to pin-pricks. All the while nobody has taken notice of my predicament I knew I should have gone back to camp. I could be raiding everyone's knapsacks right now while these fools are out searching for a frog.

I am standing motionless in the water praying for the restoration of my eyesight when all of a sudden BAM! There wasn't really a Bam, that's just for emphasis. The second my sight is restored a flash of incredible light floods the landscape and everything in our immediate vicinity has suddenly been transformed from pitched-black darkness to brilliantly colored light, as if God had flicked on some heavenly light-switch and the sun miraculously and suddenly appeared in the sky. At that very instant five young boys are mouthing in unison..."WTF!?" The transition for me is slightly more intense as I assess my situation thusly, "Oh, great. My eyesight is restored at the very moment the Ruskies have dropped a 3 megatonne bomb on us. Wait a minute! This is BFE, Louisiana. Not even the Ruskies are that stupid!"

The colors of the pond and the lush vegetation encircling it were dazzlingly vibrant in an array of hues, in such intensity as to make Monet blush...only brighter, much brighter, searingly bright!! (yeah, I know. "Searingly" It's a made-up word. I do that occasionally when no real word exists that fits the exact feeling or intensity of a situation) In any event, I'd never witnessed such color before or since. We must have looked like a family of Meerkats standing there wide-eyed, mouths agape in disbelief and wonderment. Then a bright glow of light flickered for an instant then dimmed, appearing only as the glow of a half-light of sorts typical of the light one sees when viewing a partial eclipse (those who have witnessed an eclipse, partial or otherwise, know of what I speak), then slowly receding rather than intensifying. It was at that moment we saw and heard, I do not recall in what order it was so sudden, but nonetheless, a giant ball of fire filled the sky. We watched in astonishment as this galactic display unfolded before us. The distinct sounds of flames crackling, licking the cool night air, as a blazing trail of fire is streaming behind.

I do not know if I imagined it or sensed it, but my memory recalls a sensation, a feeling of heat from the broiling object upon my face as it passed over us in the night sky. So close in fact was it that hissing sounds could also be heard. Angry popping noises as gasses were suddenly bursting free from the molten interior in defiance. The object continued across the sky a twisting, writhing ball of flame filled with fury and agony, as if sensing its end was drawing near... it hurled madly against the black sky and then... then... "WTH?"....And then, it disappeared behind the tree line. I wanted to call out, "Wait! Stop! Don't go!" But that would've have been unbelievably stupid! Yet, there was so much more I wanted to see and to know. However, the flaming object's course could not be altered or swayed. It had crossed the untold miles of the universe on its way to a final destination and inevitable destruction and nothing could modify or alter its course.

Immediately a shroud of darkness fell over us once again and we stood there momentarily suspended in a soundless vacuum (is there another sort of vacuum?) Suffice it to say it was quiet, like that moment just before a Sasquatch shows up. Our minds raced to process, sort, and file all the sounds and images we had just witnessed. All at once we were blabbing in unison, exclaiming our perceptions concerning the mysterious object. What was it? Was it the End of the World? Was it a

Martian Attack? (The movie, "War of the Worlds", based on the book of the same name by H. G. Wells, had been released a couple of years earlier. In the movie the Martian invasion was engineered by the use of giant fireballs which carried the Martians and their vehicles to earth.)

All at once our clamor was stifled by the sound of a muffled yet thundering, B-O-O-M!" that shook the ground under our feet, signaling the fireball's end as it's reached its final destination many miles in the distance. The sound seemed to roll over us as a wave crashing onto shore and then a hush fell over the pond once again. For a few minutes we scanned the sky, searching for signs we knew not; perhaps evidence of another fireball? But there was nothing save the stillness of the night and the ever-present cathedral of heavenly lights unchanged and once again reassuring us that all was well... that in spite of the brief interlude of frantic turmoil generated by the extraterrestrial intruder, when measured against the backdrop and scale of the vastness of the firmament, it was, in actuality, a flyspeck in time.

We surmised that the object must have gone down somewhere deep in the marshes to the west and south of us in either Vermilion or Cameron Parishes. During this time, Cary had turned off his monster spotlight; however, the rest of us still had our flashlights turned on. Each of us began to sweep our immediate area as we prepared to return to camp. Cary was still standing atop the ring levee when a loud grunt could be heard. It sounded as though it was coming from the opposite side of the pond. The grunt was sufficient to get everyone's attention and freezing us in our tracks. This sound was not typical of the sounds we generally heard in the woods.

"What was that?" I offered inquisitively. At the very moment when we were beginning to think it was an imaginary occurrence there was yet another grunt, this one louder than the first. Cary switched on his big-boy light and scanned the opposite bank of the pond. All we could see was the impenetrable mist that floated above the water. Cary swept the far bank again and this time his light detected some slight movement in the mist. Another grunt louder than the previous two served to rivet us in our tracks.

Cary was "spot on" literally as a shadowy figure began to materialize out of the mist. I could not believe my eyes. A creature the size of a small building was ascending the opposite ring levee. It was gargantuan in size and there was this terrible odor, as if...well, let's just leave it as terrible. When the thing reached the top of the ring levee it stopped. I could see it was covered in long grey hair, all over its body except for the face. It had black eyes and a cone shape head, and all I could think of was King Kong's baby brother. Through all this, none of us dared move. Cary put his hi-beam directly on the creature's face...which seemed to instantly piss it off. It opened its mouth and let out a roar that I swear resonated so deep in my chest as to make it feel as though the sound was emanating from inside me. I had never felt such a feeling ever before. When he opened his mouth he had a mouth full of square teeth, like a horse. He made a move, a step as if preparing to step down off the levee in our direction. Somebody, everybody I'm uncertain...shouted in unison "RUN!" I swear this sounds crazy, but I remember thinking of Mantan Moreland, the comic, actor of the 1940's who used to proclaim every time he faced danger, "Feets! Do yo' duty!" Then he'd run like the wind in the opposite direction. A real comic moment...which this definitely was not!

I ran headlong into the terrible woods that, just moments ago, I had lamented having to transverse. The creature was now in pursuit and running in my rubber boots only made me clumsy and ineffectual as a runner. It was every man for himself and I watched Cary breeze by me as if he were running on air, his big-boy light abandoned. I could hear the monster grunting with each step he took as he seemed to draw closer to us, with each footfall he grunted Hunh, hunh, hunh, hunh... and on he came. I was bruised, scratched and bleeding and running out of air as well as my boots. When you're that terrified the body consumes a lot of air needed for the energy you expel.

I tripped over some roots and went down hard, slamming onto my belly and then sliding down a gentle slope into a ditch partially filled with water. I had no sooner come to a rest when I felt the crushing blow from a rubber heel in the middle of my back. One of my team members, no doubt running for his life, had stepped on me causing what air my lungs held to be expelled. I gasped at the impact. I could hear the creature running behind me, more like thrashing behind me ripping and tearing the flora as he came. I knew I could not get up and run again as he would've been upon me in the matter of a steps or two. I tried my best to become one with the woods, hoping he hadn't seen me go down.

I became conscious of my breathing and sensed it would give me away if I didn't get control of it. I thought my lungs might explode, but I couldn't permit my body to breathe as much as it needed to. I held my breath pushing my face into the soft damp soil in an effort to disguise or hide my breathing. The creature had stopped running as well I could hear his breathing, he was very close now. Then he made some guttural sounds, as if speaking to...? Oh, my god! Was there another creature? I was so terrified that I couldn't even cry at that moment, but I pissed my pants. I prayed. Oh! How I prayed that God would let me survive this ordeal. I could hear voices crying out in the distance. They seemed to be a long way off...team members I guessed.

The creature hadn't moved a muscle. What was he waiting for? He must not have seen me or he would've certainly been on me by now. It was then that I heard the footfalls of another being heading my way. Heaven help me; there *were* two of these things. The first one had been waiting for re-enforcements, I guess. The second beast barked at the first one as if scolding him. The first beast let out a low moan almost a whimper.

As beast two arrived on the scene I was confronted by the most awful odor one could imagine; a smell of rotting carcasses and waste material...it was enough to make a buzzard gag. I fought the overwhelming urge to vomit. My stomach was churning and my salivary glands tingled as my mouth was suddenly filled with slaver. I swallowed, and swallowed again, I would not permit myself the luxury of puking, for it would have meant my certain death.

The creatures were quiet now except for their heavy breathing. As they stood there, I sensed that they sensed my presence somehow and were waiting for me to reveal my location. Each grunted several times as if frustrated. My God, I thought, they're practically on top of me. There was some shuffling of feet as if they might be turning about to look around, and to scan their field of vision. Then I heard them sniffing, sniffing the air. Oh my God, they can smell me, I feared, however, I was somewhat relieved by the realization that I hadn't yet bathed that day and that I had, in the course of the day's activities, adorned my body with all sorts of outdoor fragrances such as sweat, river water, mud, bovine, and no-telling what-all? I prayed they would mask my presence... blot-out my human smell. I hadn't moved a muscle since falling and... God permitting I wasn't going to either.

One creature took a step and I felt the ground beneath me tremble. I prayed he wouldn't step on me because that would've been my death, as I figured he must have weighed near a thousand pounds or more. Then there was another step and another and more trembling of earth beneath me. Fortunately, when I slid into the ditch I must have rolled as I was lying in the ditch parallel with it. Had I landed across the ditch perpendicular to it I am certain I would've been discovered by then.

Suddenly there was a loud, angry growl that once again resonated deep in my chest. One beast moved my way and stopped. I heard water splashing and I thought, oh no he's in the ditch. I waited for the inevitable, but it didn't come. I then heard a slurping sound and raising my eyes only I could see a beast kneeling a few feet away from me drinking water. My god, he was the most enormous thing I've ever seen. I watched him lower his massive head to the water's edge and then, pursing his lips he then sucked water into his mouth. He must've taken in three or four mouthfuls, swallowing each one. Then he abruptly raised his head staring ahead in the direction he was facing. For a moment I was sure he had heard me make some noise and he was listening intently for another sound. The other beast now barked and the drinker then stood upright again, still gazing off in the distance. I knew that because while I could only see just above his ankles his feet never moved. I wondered just how good his peripheral vision was. I didn't even blink.

The other beast grunted a series of guttural sounds and then the drinker grunted back. I realized they were speaking to one another. The drinker abandoned his gaze and then returned to where the other was standing. A moment later they commenced ripping up trees and vegetation and thrashing about. I remember thinking... Now they're *really* pissed! I heard wood cracking and a shuffling sound. Still I didn't move and I don't know how I managed to hold my breath for that long, but I did.

There was another angry roar as if in frustration. As if saying, "I'll get you next time you little bastard!" I remember thinking there'd be no chance of that happening unless they were to start making house-calls, 'cause if I survived this encounter I would never-ever be in the woods again...*ever*! Then suddenly I heard what sounded like *another* creature off in the distance behind us, but much farther away. It seemed to be calling out. My guys gave out a couple of whoops and then I heard and felt them as they began to walk away smashing their way through the woods, 'Thump, thump, thump!" I lay there not moving or breathing for the longest time. When I was certain they had moved off, I rose up on my elbows and took a life-saving huge breath of air. I lay there for a minute or two relaxing and enjoying the new-found pleasure of taking a simple breath of air. Several minutes passed as I oxygenated my weary body. Then, pulling my arms back on either side of me I placed the palms of my hands on the ground and with my remaining strength, I pushed the upper portion of my body as if attempting a push-up, but only to point where I could peek over the ditch line. I didn't see or hear a thing. I stayed in that position to be certain they were not around, then I ever so slowly rose to a crouched position, listening for a moment before straightening myself erect. I hoped with that last effort I would not find they were standing nearby waiting for me to make a gesture such as this. Nothing happened.

From the ditch I crept slowly, measuring each step. I was barefooted now having run out of my boots and my socks. By the time I had worked my way slowly and quietly through the densely covered terrain, taking care not to trip on some bramble, the soles of my feet were raw. It had taken quite some time to reach the gravel road and I was totally exhausted physically and emotionally. I sat in the middle of the road contemplating my next move. I patted down my body to see if there was anything crawling on me. As I did so I realized I had the sense to put my flashlight inside my pants pocket. I did not recall doing so, but I was thankful to have it. I decided I would wait for daylight to leave the woods, but after a while I began to hear rustling in the brush. Even though I reasoned it to be that of small mammals, rodents or the like, I was, nonetheless, beginning to get anxious about spending the remainder of the night in the dark of the road. Finally I decided it was safe to turn on my light. Retrieving it from my pocket I said a little prayer that it would shine for me and luckily...it did!

I could see instantly that my eight-legged friends had been busy as usual and had spun their labyrinth of webbing across the road for me, thank-you-very-much! But by now I was absolutely fearless. I just took my time weaving and dodging my way between them, cursing now and then as a foot came down hard on the gravel. Finally I broke out into the coming of a new day. It was already light but the sun was not up yet. I stood in the middle of Saloon Road looking back at the dense woods I had at long last finally emerged.

The pavement under me feet was still cool and the rough texture of asphalt felt good to my bruised and aching feet. I had survived...God had let me live to see at least another day. Smiling in satisfaction, I turned to continue my journey home. Just then, off in the distance, I heard what sounded like a couple of whoops. That was all the encouragement I needed. C'mon, Mantan, I moaned as I sprinted (well maybe sprinted is an exaggeration) quickly limped was more like it. The asphalt didn't offer the comfort I first felt upon my extraction from the woods as the bumpy surface was now harsh and unforgiving on my bruised and bloody feet. Fortunately, it wasn't a great distance before I reached Poplar camp road. Crossing over the cattle guard that stretched across the entrance I trekked the short distance to the camp house. I wondered how the rest of the team had endured the evening. Nearing the camp I saw several pickup trucks and a handful of Sheriff Deputy's vehicles parked on the front lawn. Opening the camp door you could've heard a pin-drop as a room full of astonished looking faces gawked at my entrance. I just looked at them and said, "WHAT?!"

It wasn't long after I found myself being treated by a couple of ambulance attendants who cleaned and treated most of my wounds before strapping me onto their gurney in preparation for loading me into an ambulance. By this time my parents had arrived and my mother was practically hysterical. One look at me and she broke down sobbing and all she wanted to do was hug and kiss my battered face, which by now was really swollen and bruised and was terribly sensitive to touch, even a mother's. I pleaded "Mom I'm alright, it's okay." She couldn't respond verbally she just nodded her head in agreement, her cheeks washed with streams of tears. Finally, my dad took her by the elbow and gently led her away so they could finish loading me into the ambulance. The ride to the hospital seemed to take forever but the driver, not wanting to jostle my fragile frame, deliberately drove slower since I was not in a life threatening condition. I was at the ER for several hours for treatment and interviews with medical personnel, law enforcement authorities, and news crews. Later, I was permitted a short debriefing of sorts with my team mates who all survived the ordeal with minor cuts and abrasions. It was late afternoon before I was able to convince the doctors I was well enough to go home.

By the time I arrived back home I was drained. While my mom busied herself in the kitchen cooking I was washing the wood-funk from my body in a long, hot shower. Standing in front of the full-length mirror I was able to take assessment of my body damage. I was hideous. My face was badly swollen and disfigured. Bruises, cuts, and abrasions literally covered my body and walking was incredibly painful as my feet had ballooned to the size of clown feet. I was a wreck, but I was alive! Fortunately, I had suffered only minor injuries, no major damage or broken bones, a miracle to say the least. After showering I enjoyed a hot meal of sausage, eggs, grits and buttered biscuits. I was ravenous. As I mopped up the last of the yolk with a bite of biscuit, my dad announced that what I needed most at that time was a good night's rest and that any other talking could be done in the morning.

While I was enjoying my breakfast meal mom was stripping and remaking my bed with clean linens. She stayed long enough to tuck me in and place a glass of cool water on my bedside table before gently kissing my face. Lightly brushing my hair back as mother's will do she told me how much she loved me while tears welled up in her eyes again. Taking her hand in mine, I assured her that I was fine I just needed some sleep. It felt heavenly lying on those cool sheets. Dad had set the air to a perfect temperature and the hum of the compressor was a soothing sound in my ears. I stretched my weary, aching body to the point of pain before relaxing it. I wanted to sleep so badly, but I was still wired from the experience and its follow-up. I wondered what kind of stir the events might create in the morning.

My thoughts darted about like a house fly and I made a deliberate decision to reflect only on the object in the sky rather than the monsters since the fireball was less odious. I deliberated about the Martians and their crash landing. There was gonna be hell to pay for someone... whoever the idiot navigator was that charted their course to land in the vast marshes of south Louisiana. "I pity da' fool!" I chuckled. I calculated at their speed the fireball could've been buried under several deposits of muck and mire. By the time the Martians finally dug out, they'd have to contend with gators and marsh mosquitoes. Oh, yeah... the marsh skeeters... there won't be a drop of...? I paused and wondered if Martians have blood? No matter, I thought.

We wouldn't have to worry much over their failed invasion. Besides, even if they were lucky enough to overcome the odds of gators and skeeters, they'd still have to contend with the Cajun population who wouldn't take lightly to the disruption of their beloved marshes by a horde of ugly little aliens and who would, in all probability, take great pride in harvesting as many Martians as possible. Certainly everyone would want a Martian mount to hang in their den. Yep! It was gonna be a rude awakening for the Martians and any other cosmic invaders... I envisioned the little green guys fighting off hordes of swamp people as wave after wave of pissed-off Cajuns in airboats, armed to the teeth rained death and destruction down on them. Don't leave your death rays behind boys, you're gonna need 'em.

It had been an exhausting weekend to say the very least. Yet there would be no dreams of huge spiders, or of a Martian invasion, or of monstrous monsters lurking in the deep woods that would threaten my slumber. I smiled contentedly, All was well… that end's well, I thought. I closed my eyes and slept like a baby.

I am a long way from that awful night in the woods so many years ago. True to my vow, I haven't been in the woods ever since that night. I'm certain each of us in our own way holds onto some recollection of the phenomenon that occurred in the sky and in the woods that dark summer night. It was not a night forgotten easily and, we all have had to deal with it on our own terms. I still have nightmares, but not as often. The creatures we saw that night are still out there…somewhere, of that I am certain. Sometimes, in a quiet moment, I'll wonder...wonder if they ever think of me...the one that stumbled yet managed to flee? Hmm. I wonder...?

Fini

TALES FROM THE
CRYPTID LIBRARY

The following short narratives are encounters that have occurred on our residential property during the past five years and I make no apology for the manner in which they are written as they have been transcribed exactly as they happened without embellishment.

Apparition Occurrences-

Shadow People Encounter
Date & Time:
18 Sep 2015, 4:00am
Place:
Residence

On the above date I awoke from my sleep around 3:30am to go use the bathroom. From there I proceeded to the kitchen to get something to drink. After slaking my thirst, and realizing I was fully awake I decided to go to my gun room, a small room located just beyond the wash room where I stored my gun collection. Inside was enough room for a chair and table and a small work bench where I cleaned and did simple repairs on firearms. My motivation was to complete preparations of certain weapons and accoutrement that my friend Walt was taking to his eldest son who had recently purchased them from me. Walt and his wife, Stephanie had been our guests for a week and they were scheduled to depart in a couple of days for their home in Chattanooga, TN.

At roughly 4am, I was seated in my chair in the gun room at my work table. Hanging over the door opening was a large Battle Flag that served as a barrier, blocking a viewer from seeing into the room when it was not lighted. The overhead lights to the gun room and the adjoining washroom were both on as was a large lamp atop of the kitchen refrigerator.

Some time had passed and I was still seated at my work table when I heard two snapping sounds emanating from the kitchen area. The sounds were sufficiently loud enough to draw my attention away from my task momentarily. I paused to listen further, but as there were no other noises I turned back to my work. Moments later the same snapping sounds occurred again and I was fully conscious of the noises in the kitchen and more importantly, what or who was the cause of these sounds. It was not a natural occurrence, once perhaps, twice, very unlikely. The thought entered my mind that we might have vermin in the house and I muttered aloud, "Damn rats!"

reflecting on an unpleasant episode that occurred many years past when we had a rat invasion in our home. It had been quite an ordeal ridding the house of them and the thought of another rat encounter was unsettling and occupied my thoughts.

By now I was contemplating r contemplating what course of action I should take when, quite suddenly, out of the corner of my eye I became conscious of the shadow of a person peering into the gun room door and it seemed as though the flag fluttered momentarily in such a way as it would if someone were actually entering the gunroom, at least that's how I recall it. At first glance I assumed it was my wife who had risen from her sleep and was coming to check on my whereabouts. It was at that moment that I spoke to whomever it was, uttering a weak and somewhat annoyed, "He-e-e-y?" The dark outline of the figure stood motionless at the threshold of the door looking at me momentarily through the flag before pulling back. I thought it strange behavior for my wife to not respond when spoken to.

I rolled my chair toward the door and the figure, and as I drew nearer to it, the figure retreated from the doorway back towards the kitchen door opening. At this point I had rolled my chair to where I was seated just inside the gun room looking through the flag. There, standing in the kitchen doorway no more than four feet from me was a small, shadowy, humanoid figure. For a fleeting moment we just stared at one another in disbelief, well I was in disbelief, as for the figure, who knows? Then it advanced towards me slowly, and as it approached it came into the light of the wash room where I could see quite clearly a dark outline of a humanoid, but I did not observe any discernible features...merely an outline or a shadow of a person.

That moment when it stood in the kitchen door staring at me it seemed to be considering its options. Why I say that I don't know except that it seemed to be the logical response given the circumstances. I was riveted to my chair and the situation most definitely called for someone to make a move. The figure was the logical choice. It advanced toward me gliding as it were silently past me, as if floating on air, and continued out of my line of sight towards the door at the opposite end of the wash room leading outside. In the few moments it took for the apparition to pass by me I had the distinct impression that I had struck fear in it because it seemed to cower as it passed me hugging the wall as it turned towards the rear door.

For an instant I gazed into its featureless face, no more than an arms-length away and I sensed it may have been a child because of its diminutive size. I later measured the space it occupied as it passed by me taking note that the top of its head reached no further than the bottom of the frame of a picture hanging on the opposite wall. By my calculation the figure was no taller than 5-feet, probably less. Immediately after it had passed from my view I was fixed in utter bewilderment of the scene I had just witnessed and I murmured to myself "WTF was *THAT*?!"

I instantly arose from my chair brushing the flag aside in the process while peering to my left at the rear door. The door was closed and bolted. Had something or someone turned the dead-bolt, opened and closed the door, resetting the dead-bolt in the process I don't know how I would have missed seeing it, or at the very least heard it. The figure had disappeared. I walked to the door, turned the dead-bolt and opened it. Then, stepping out into the early morning darkness I was aware of an eerie quietness, a stillness which seemed to stifle any chance of sound similar to standing outdoors after a heavy snowfall.

Remembering the passage in Jude where reference is made to the Book of Enoch when the Archangel Michael rebuked Satan when contending with him over the body of Moses, I uttered the words, "The Lord rebukes you!" Then added, "Go and never return." I walked back inside closing and re-bolting the deadbolt. Seated once again in my chair in the gun room I replayed the event in my mind slowly pondering each detail in my mind's eye, recalling exactly the sequence of events as they occurred.

I stared through the flag and it was then that I processed the height of the figure to be no taller than 5 feet because as I stated previously I made a mental notation carefully observing where the top of its head was in relation to the picture hanging behind it as it moved past me towards the back door. I also revisited my impression as it slid past me, hugging the wall as if to insure there would be no physical contact between us should I attempt to reach out to it. Musing over that thought I chuckled to myself as I was quite certain that I was in no danger of doing something that foolish.

Needless to say, I was not the least bit sleepy. I went into the kitchen and fixed a large pot of coffee which I proceeded to drink alone with my thoughts. Had I been the least bit sleepy after the event the eight cups of coffee had sufficiently removed any possibility of sleepiness. I checked the kitchen area for any evidence my caller might have left behind and searched for the item that might have caused the snapping sounds. Everything was as it should be, nothing was disturbed and I was perplexed that I could not discover the source of the clicking/snapping sounds. I thought of the "Terminator" movies and the sounds that accompanied the teleporting of Terminators between dimensions in time travel.

I do not believe the shadow person had been in the house for any period of time and I am firmly of the opinion that the snapping sounds I heard were associated with the entity's appearance, although I can offer no real, or tangible proof of that. It is simply a deep seated feeling I have about how it happened to manifest itself in my house.

Later that day, about mid-morning, I recounted the experience to Walt in detail noting his deportment in which he received my tale with obvious skepticism. Nonetheless, I've recorded those details here as best my memory serves me of that eerie occurrence early on that September morning in 2015.

Dogman (Rougarou) Encounter

Date & Time:
24 or 25th February 2019, 9:00pm
Outside
Residence

I have a detached office, a man cave of sorts not 10-paces out a back door in our master bedroom. A small flagstone patio connects the house with this structure. The office is 20' X 12' and its exterior is covered with weathered board and batten and a corrugated metal roof. Immediately behind the office is a storage shed of similar construction, roughly 12' X 14'. A concrete walk skirts the office and connects the patio with the shed's entrance.

This shed has been a home for rat snakes, dozens of field mice and rats as well as a contingency of wayward neighborhood cats. Add to that the occasional family of raccoons and opossum and you have all the ingredients necessary for a rousing and rambunctious evening of feisty fauna festivities. I should also mention there are two live Oak trees, one on either side of the shed that anchor it to the northeast corner of my property. Beyond that point lies spotted woodlands dotted by intermittent open areas and numerous residences.

2/10ths of a mile beyond that corner lies the Vermilion River, a sluggish stream more reminiscent of a bayou, as it was once known. On either side of it are expansive areas with thick hardwoods. There is also found along both sides of this waterway all manner and types of construction from commercial to residential as well as some camps in the more remote ares.

Back to my office and shed. I had installed flood lights at the corner of the shed facing the concrete walk. These lights are activated by motion detectors that enable me to be aware of any activity occurring between my office and the shed. I am a commercial artist/graphics designer and author and I do a lot of my work at night and there had been those evenings when there had been a spirited commotion of nightlife occurring on the roof of my office and adjoining shed.

I have also been an armchair cryptozoologist for some time now. I grew up in rural South Louisiana and spent many years in the woods hunting, fishing, trapping, camping... you name it, but until having bi-lateral knee replacements this past summer, I'd spent the previous 15-

years restricted to a life conducive to indoor activities rather than outdoors.

My studies had led me to a conclusion that some Dogmen are more spiritual than physical. I also am of the opinion that if you want to see one of these creatures badly enough, you will. There is a conduit between the spirit world or dimension and our plane. I don't know how...a portal of some sort? I also had an encounter with shadow people in my home back in 2015. In addition, I had also heard it said that Dogmen have the habit of walking on the roofs of buildings, houses primarily, in which people are living. Now, if you distill all of this information it leads to my Dogman encounter which is as follows.

Over the period of several weeks I began hearing different sounds emanating from the roof of my office much heavier footsteps, not the scurrying sounds of 4-footed, arboreal creatures, but heavy steps of a bi-pedal nature. The sounds occurred only at night and typically commenced about 15-minutes after entering my office. Sometimes the racket was a bit unnerving and sufficiently distracting that it has caused me to leave my work early.

On those nights I walked back to my house feeling as though eyes were following my movements, penetrating the darkness beyond the pitch of my roof. As unsettling as these events were I had restrained the urge to rush into the house as I did not want to send a signal of flight or fight and risk provoking an encounter...Therefore, I would consciously assume an air of indifference, as if that were possible, more to calm my nerves I suppose, but nonetheless, I would walk nonchalantly if you will up the patio as if oblivious to the commotion on the roof.

This routine continued for a several weeks; loud thumping sounds from an object of considerable weight walking bi-pedially back and forth across the roof. Sometimes it seemed as though my visitor might crash through the roof, the noise was so great. I didn't want to go outside to investigate for fear of eliciting an encounter; which was exactly what I feared this being was attempting to do. I hoped that with time it would tire of its attempts to lure me out or goad me into a confrontation.

On what would be the last night of these nocturnal visitations I was once again attempting to complete some cartoons I had been working on for sometime. I had been in my office a short time when suddenly a thunderous, "Boom! Boom! Boom!", on the roof. I must be honest that it startled me so I almost fell out of my chair. This was far more aggressive than anything I had experienced thus far and I took this deliberate act as a response to my ignoring it. The very thing I had sought to avoid I had inadvertently provoked by manner of annoyance. This being or entity was not going to be ignored as it seemed to want me to take notice of it in some way.

I stood up from my computer desk and listened as it stomped across the roof. I walked over to my office door, hesitating momentarily before opening it then quickly stepping outside. However, once outside I remained under the roof or portico overhang covering the entrance of my office. It was deathly quiet. Not a sound. No dogs barking in the distance no crickets or peepers just an unearthly and eerie silence; a silence likened to one stepping outside after a heavy snowfall. I stepped back inside my office and retrieved my Sig P245, checking the chamber to confirm that a round was seated snuggly in the breach. I am an excellent shot and have practiced defensive tactics with pistols and was quite certain I could place three shots into the mouth of this thing. My Sig had a full magazine of 185-grain Cor-bon ammo, a hot load by any standard.

I heard light movement from above as if my caller was shifting its weight and positioning itself. I was quite certain that it was now in a place where it could pounce on me as soon as I was fully exposed. Before stepping outside I prayed that God would protect me and deliver me unscathed from this encounter. Once again I opened the door, but this time I took care to not make a sound. I stepped over the threshold, reciting the 23rd Psalm, "Yea, though I walk through.." and confirming that the Lord would protect me from whatever was about to happen.

Standing under the cover of the portico I took a deep breath and removed the Sig from my coat pocket. I drew the hammer back in a firing position and held the pistol on my chest on my heart which was beating like a Hummingbird's. It was only then that I noticed my flood lights covering the walk to the shed were not on and that concerned me deeply. Committed to seeing this effort through I stepped cautiously to a point at which I was then out from under the protective cover of the portico's roof. I quickly spun around, my Sig in a firing position, both arms extended and holding my pistol in both hands for balance. Scanning the roof I determined there was no immediate threat.

I then side stepped to my right placing me at a point where I was standing at the railing that runs alongside the patio. I turned slowly to look in the direction of the walkway and the shed, a move that would have forced me to lean awkwardly over the railing. I had no sooner begun to perform that maneuver when I was jolted upright by a snarl which I can only describe as something emitted by a Hound from Hell! I know snarls and growls, but this was no dog. No dog taking breath of life could have created such a frighteningly menacing and evil sound.

LINK- Go to the 00:51sec mark. This is very close to the sound I heard that night)

https://youtu.be/dvHHi3GI1XU

I had what I call a Mantan Moreland moment. If you're familiar with the great comic actor whose most endearing words were, "Feet's...do yo' duty!", whenever he was startled by sudden danger. Looking no further and avoiding eye contact I immediately pivoted heal and toe to my right towards the door of my house. And this time, abandoning all casualness, I rushed up the patio as fast as possible fearing to glance behind me to see whatever was lurking there in the dark. Closing and locking the door behind me I could only ponder what I had just experienced. I let out a deep breath. What if that beast hadn't snarled and given warning of its presence? What if I hadn't stopped my effort to investigate the walkway? I considered myself very fortunate.

The next day I was reliving the events of the previous night. I began to analyze them as they occurred and discovered to my surprise that when I thought the beast was positioning itself on the roof it was in fact climbing down or leaping from the roof. Once down it stood on the walk to the storage shed. From this vantage point it could in the pitch of night (the floodlights being out as I mentioned previously) look through the office window and observe everything I was doing, which included the "racking" of my Sig.

Discovering I was armed it no doubt decided that any overt actions on its part would likely end up with it sustaining wounds or worse. In light of this it had no choice but to abort contact with me. Especially since it appeared I might be coming down the walk where it was standing. There was no danger of me going down that walk because it was darker than the proverbial "Well-Digger's ass." Even so, the beast had no choice but to alert me of its presence. Had it not, I most assuredly would have delivered 3-Cor-bons into it in quick succession. Of course I wouldn't have survived that encounter and Mr. hair-all-over would have had one helluva headache the next day. This scenario is all conjecture on my part; however, it fits the time-line and events perfectly and logically.

Since that night threefold weeks have elapsed and there has been no more noise on my rooftop. All is quiet. All is peaceful. I have replayed these events as they occurred over and over in my mind and while I had no visual reference for this encounter I have surmised that the beast could not have been more than 8-feet from me when it snarled. I will always remember the sound of that evil growl.

I failed to mention a light aside: my backdoor neighbor has 2-yip-yaps, I call 'em... small dogs with peculiarly, hi-pitched and annoying barks. These dogs will bark at the slightest sound with little or provocation. A popcorn fart from a pissant will send them into a yapping frenzy. However, they were strangely quiet that evening; it was then I realized they had been silent every evening I experienced the noisome visitor. I hoped the visitor had perhaps taken them as a late night snack...but, no such luck, as they greeted me with a chorus of yip-yaps upon my opening my bedroom door on the way to my office the next day.

The following is a sketch of my Office/Shed layout for the reader's perusal.

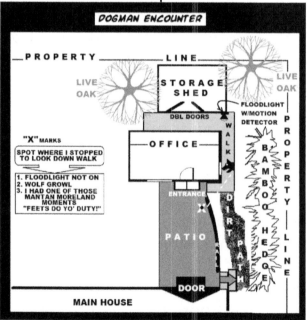

However, approximately one month from the night of my encounter I awoke around 3:00 am, as I am often won't to do, and I went into the kitchen to have a bowl of cereal. As I was draining the bowl of milk I was startled by a loud growl outside my kitchen window. I knew at once that the Rougarou was back. Note: We have quite a few dogs in our area and neighborhood which can be heard at all times during the day and early evening. However, the only dogs actually seen are on a leash during a walk. We have no loose, free-range dogs in our area. In 10-years I've never seen one.

I resisted going to the window for a look for fear I would be staring into the face of my nighttime visitor of the past. It was a mistake I later regretted, but in reality I truly wasn't prepared for an encore. I made a quick check of all the doors to satisfy myself that we were bolted and locked, and then I returned to my bed and heard no further disturbances from outside.

Lying in the dark I pondered the reasoning of this visitation. I concluded that it was a warning of sorts? Why would a dog appear suddenly and then sit under my window and make a threatening growl, identical to the one I encountered a month before? I sense he will be back and if so I want to be prepared emotionally, spiritually, and physically for his return.

Bobcat or Hellcat Encounter?

Date & Time:
Winter 2012, 10:00pm
Outside
Residence

One cold winter evening in 2012, I opened the door in our master bedroom that leads to a covered patio to retrieve a soft drink from a cooler on the opposite side of the patio. As I stepped outside, a creature to my right, suddenly burst out of a large cushioned chair and flashed across me making considerable racket accompanied by a loud, "Rowowowerr" or some-such sound a cat might make, only much louder. This creature was no house cat. I was startled to say the least, but assuming for the moment it was a neighborhood cat I continued to the cooler and retrieved a couple of sodas. Turning to go back to my bedroom, I happened to glance to my right and sitting amongst some bushes that grow against the back fence I saw the outline or silhouette of a cat, a very large cat judging from its size. I couldn't help noticing the creature possessed a pair of very large green, almost luminescent eyes that were watching me carefully. I thought it odd that the creature didn't run away after I startled it; something a house cat or Tom would've done. It just sat there looking at me as I walked past it. I entered my bedroom door and bolted it behind me. I thought the incident unusual, but I didn't ponder it until the next day as I was troubled by some of the points of the event.

Three things are noteworthy:
1. The clamor or raucous noise of the cat when startled. Most cats would have simply runoff quietly as possible.
2. The size of the figure and its large glowing green eyes.
3. And, again the fact that it did not run-away, choosing instead to remain seated a few feet away from me. Not normal cat behavior.

Spirits on Deck-

29th April 2019

Following the appearance of the Shadow Person right up to today's date there have been numerous noises, sounds, knocks thumps, bump, and voices, doors slamming, etc. inside our house. In fact as I write this in my journal a bump was heard at the door leading to my office. Investigating it proved fruitless. These bumps on my door are practically a nightly occurrence.

Just today my wife heard me calling her name. She came out to my office around 7:00am to see what I wanted with her. I informed that I had been in my office since 5:00am. I don't think she was totally convinced, but when she left my office she had a look of puzzlement on her face. I have taken to referring to these incidents as the actions of spiritual visitors, i e ghosts or disembodied spirits and so far they seem quite benign.

I just heard more noise outside my door. Anyway, I also see movements out of the corners of my eyes. Last week a figure peeking into the kitchen, but when I turn back to look there is nothing there.

Interestingly enough I have heard voices on many occasions calling out when I am in the bathroom on the pot. My "friends?" know that's a good time to draw attention to them because I'm unavailable to go and search it out. Just a couple of hours ago I was in the bathroom (no one else in the house), not using the bathroom and there was a distinct knocking, four knocks that seemed to be on a piece of furniture in the house, a table or? But it didn't have the hollow knocking sound that occurs when someone knocks on a door. Uncertain, I checked all the doors to the house anyway.

The noises seem to be getting more frequent and I have developed the habit of speaking to them. "You're welcome to stay as long as you're civil and not unruly." "They" also know I'm a believer in Jesus Christ, my Lord and Savior, and that I'll call the Holy Ghost down on them if they get out of line.

Which brings me to a point; people ask do your believe in the spiritual and supernatural? My answer, "Of course I do, I'm a Christian. My Father God is a Heavenly spirit as is His only begotten son, Jesus Christ. Then there is the Holy Spirit or Holy Ghost, along with several billion

Angels...not to mention our adversary, the devil and his legions of demons. So, does that qualify me as a believer in the spirit world? You bet your bippy it does!

Saturday, Juneteenth(15) 2019.

Today I was visited by a little girl, about my granddaughter's age (7) and a young woman (her mother?). This was one of those indirect visitations where you see the apparition only out of the corner of my eye. This was a Saturday and I was working on some drawings. I learned to see these apparitions quite well. No direct eye contact, they were there most of the day observing me and listening to me talk to myself. The little girl appeared first, but she must've grown tired of watching me.

A short time later the woman appeared and she spent most of the day watching me work. She was seated to my right, about 3-feet from me and every now and then I would verify her presence by looking away from my computer screen in a dead-zone, so to speak (pun intended) an area between my monitor and her. it was at the moments when I could see her quite clearly. I began including her in my conversations with myself because I wanted her to be aware that I was aware of her. At the end of the day I stood up and spoke to her saying something like, "Well, I'm going in now. I've finished working for this day. I'd hold the door for you, but the door is no obstacle for you, so I'll just say goodbye." Like all of my visitations, these two just made solo appearances.

Friday, May 21, 2019.
This particular evening I am baby-sitting my granddaughter, Sally as her mother is out with friends and Bubba, her grandmother, is driving for Uber. At around 7:15, Sally made a request of Alexa. I instinctively turned to see what she was doing and I saw her in the washroom, but wait that's not Sally. I leaned forward to investigate as I was seated on the sofa in the keeping room and when I did the face pulled back from the door opening. I looked at Sally to see her reaction, but she was totally unaware of what had just occurred.

I cannot help but wonder if we're not at or very near a portal to the spirit world?

ASWest
2020

Printed in Great Britain
by Amazon

41853561R00152